THIS BOOK

BELONGS TO:

. . . .

. . . .

A BEATRIX POTTER™
Treasury

She looked suspiciously at the sack and wondered
where everybody was?

A BEATRIX POTTER™
Treasury

The Original and Authorized Editions by

BEATRIX POTTER

New colour reproductions

FREDERICK WARNE

FREDERICK WARNE

UK | USA | Canada | Ireland | Australia
India | New Zealand | South Africa | China
Frederick Warne is part of the Penguin Random House group of companies
whose addresses can be found at global.penguinrandomhouse.com.

www.peterrabbit.com

This edition published 2006 by Frederick Warne
Reissued in 2016

002

Printed in China

ISBN: 978–0–241–27896–3

CONTENTS

THE STORY OF BEATRIX POTTER

Beatrix, aged 8, with her parents, Rupert and Helen Potter

Rupert Potter, a keen amateur photographer, often took pictures of Derwentwater.

BEATRIX POTTER was born in 1866 to Rupert and Helen Potter. She had a conventionally sheltered Victorian childhood and was educated at home by governesses. Beatrix's well-to-do parents disapproved of her forming friendships with children of her own age, so she had a somewhat lonely childhood. Though she was not allowed to mix with her peers, Beatrix met many famous artists, politicians and thinkers when they came to visit her father. For companionship, Beatrix and her younger brother filled the nursery with numerous pets of all varieties. At one stage, the menagerie consisted of a green frog, two lizards, some water newts, a snake and a rabbit, all of which were carefully studied by the children. From an early age Beatrix drew everything around her, and covered pages with sketches of animals. Her childhood sketchbooks feature fantasy pictures of animals engaged in human activities, such as rabbits ice skating and wearing clothes.

From the age of 16 Beatrix Potter took most of her summer holidays in the Lake District with her family. They often stayed on the shores of Derwentwater, a lake popular with many sportsmen, photographers and painters. Beatrix loved Derwentwater from her first visit. She climbed the fells around the lake and went out to the four little islands in the middle. She walked in the woods by the shore, watching the squirrels there, and observed the rabbits in the gardens of the houses where she stayed. She filled little notebooks with her

watercolour sketches of the surrounding landscapes. Beatrix also loved the picturesque village of Near Sawrey, 'I was very sorry to come away in spite of the broken weather. It is as nearly perfect a little place as I ever lived in, and such nice old-fashioned people in the village.' So charmed was she by this Lake District village that Beatrix determined to make it her home one day. Beatrix's skill as an artist was evident to everyone who saw her drawings and with the encouragement of her Uncle Henry who suggested that she might try selling some drawings for a little income, Beatrix began work on six whimsical designs using her pet rabbit as her model. They were bought for £6 by the publisher Hildesheimer & Faulkner, who asked to see more of her work. Beatrix was delighted. Some of the designs were published as Christmas and New Year cards in 1890. At the age of 24, Beatrix had begun her professional career. The earning of her own money was a source of great comfort to Beatrix, who had always dreamed of being independent.

Beatrix Potter enjoyed writing letters to children, and it was in these letters that she began to write and illustrate her stories. A picture letter dated 4th September 1893 (see overleaf) was the origin of *The Tale of Peter Rabbit*. The letter was sent to Noel Moore, who was the son of Beatrix's ex-governess, when he was ill in bed. It told the story of a disobedient rabbit named Peter, and it has become one of the most quoted and famous letters ever written. A few years later, it occurred to Beatrix Potter that she might make a little book out of the story. She wrote to ask if Noel had kept the letter, and if so could she borrow it? Noel had kept the letter, and was glad to lend it to her.

Above, left: Beatrix observed her pet rabbits' behaviour and painted them in different positions.

Above, right: One of Beatrix's Christmas card designs, published in 1890

Noel Moore

Above and right: Beatrix Potter's picture letter to Noel Moore, sent from Scotland in 1893

and the other shoe amongst the potatoes. After losing them he ran on four legs & went faster, so that I think he would

have got away altogether, if he had not unfortunately run into a gooseberry net and got caught fast by the large buttons on his jacket. It was a blue jacket with brass buttons; quite new.

Mr McGregor came up with a basket which he intended to pop on the top of Peter, but Peter wriggled out just in time, leaving his jacket behind,

and this time he found the gate, slipped underneath and ran home safely.

Mr McGregor hung up the little jacket & shoes for a scarecrow, to frighten the black birds.

Peter was ill during the evening, in consequence of over eating himself. His mother put him to bed and gave him a dose of camomile tea,

but Flopsy, Mopsy, and Cottontail had bread and milk and blackberries for supper.   I am coming back to London next Thursday, so I hope I shall see you soon, and the new baby.   I remain, dear Noel, yours affectionately
                    Beatrix Potter.

Canon Hardwicke
Rawnsley

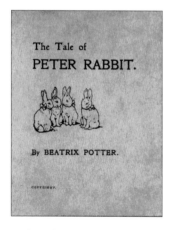

A first edition copy of
The Tale of Peter Rabbit,
privately printed in 1901

Canon Hardwicke Rawnsley, a friend of the Potter family and their local vicar in the Lake District, was the author of a popular collection of moral poems for children. With his help, the manuscript of *The Tale of Peter Rabbit* was sent to at least six publishers. Incredible though it now seems, one by one, these publishers rejected it! Undaunted, Beatrix had 250 copies of her story printed privately and those that she did not give away as presents she sold for 1/2d. Meanwhile, Beatrix and Canon Rawnsley continued to search for a commercial publisher for the book. Frederick Warne & Co. was interested in publishing the story, but strongly felt that colour illustrations were needed. Initially, Beatrix was against using colour, feeling it would be too expensive and also citing the 'rather uninteresting colour of a good many of the subjects which are most of them rabbit brown and green'. Once they persuaded Beatrix to use colour, Warne agreed to publish the story in 1902.

As in all her Tales, Beatrix used simple, direct language and never patronised her young readers.

She tested out her prose on friends' children and responded to their requests. Much of the appeal of her Tales comes from their blend of light relief and serious undertones. Though most of the stories have happy endings, the characters do suffer the consequences of their actions: Peter, for instance, goes to bed with a stomach ache as a result of over-indulgence in Mr. McGregor's garden. Many letters were exchanged between Beatrix and her publishers, her strong character emerging in the correspondence as the book progressed. Beatrix was interested in all aspects of book production. She had decided, informed opinions about everything from price and design, to format and the quality of the colour printing. Beatrix wanted the book to be as cheap as possible, so that children could afford to buy it with their pocket money. She was equally emphatic that the book be small, to accommodate little hands.

By the end of 1903 over 50,000 copies of *The Tale of Peter Rabbit* had been sold. 'The public must be fond of rabbits!' wrote Beatrix. 'What an appalling quantity of Peter.' *The Tale of Peter Rabbit* is as appealing today as when the story was first published, and Beatrix had a theory to explain its success. She wrote in 1905, 'It is much more satisfactory to address a real live child; I often think that that was the secret of the success of Peter Rabbit, it was written to a child— not made to order.' A keen businesswoman, Beatrix paid close attention to what her audience wanted and looked for ways to capitalise on her popular creations. Soon after *The Tale of Peter Rabbit* was published, she began to make a Peter Rabbit doll. 'I am cutting out calico patterns of Peter, I have not got it right yet, but the expression is going to be lovely; especially the whiskers—(pulled out of a brush!).' She registered her doll at the Patent Office in London on 28th December 1903. The doll was followed the next year by wallpaper and then a Peter Rabbit board game devised by Beatrix herself.

There has been much speculation about the setting for the story, but Beatrix herself did not know for sure which location had inspired her when she wrote the picture letter to Noel. In a letter written in 1942, she wrote, 'Peter was so composite and scattered in locality that I have found it troublesome to explain its various sources . . .' But although there is not one specific local setting for the story, the real Peter Rabbit, who was Beatrix's pet, is well known. Beatrix's rabbit, Peter Piper, lived to be nine years old and used to stretch out in front of the fire on the hearth rug like a cat. Beatrix never forgot the hero of her first little book.

Beatrix's Peter Rabbit doll had lead shot inside its feet to make it stand upright.

A watercolour of Peter Rabbit, painted in 1899

In one of her privately printed copies of *The Tale of Peter Rabbit* she wrote, 'In affectionate remembrance of poor old Peter Rabbit . . . whatever the limitations of his intellect or shortcomings of his fur, and his ears and toes, his disposition was uniformly amiable and his temper unfailingly sweet. An affectionate companion and a quiet friend.'

Beatrix Potter spent the summer of 1903 at Fawe Park, a large country house with a beautiful garden on the shore of Derwentwater. Soon after she arrived, she sent her editor, Norman Warne, a draft of what she called 'the rabbit story', a sequel to the *The Tale of Peter Rabbit*. Beatrix Potter modelled the hero of *The Tale of Benjamin Bunny* on her first pet rabbit, who had been smuggled into the nursery in a paper bag. His name was Benjamin H. Bouncer, or Bounce for short, and he was very fond of hot buttered toast and sweets. She described him as 'a noisy, cheerful determined animal, inclined to attack strangers'. *The Tale of Benjamin Bunny* continued the exploits of Peter Rabbit, who had wandered into Mr. McGregor's garden and very nearly ended up in a pie. Now, joined by his self-possessed cousin Benjamin, Peter sets out to recover his lost clothes from the scarecrow in the garden and has many adventures on the way.

A few weeks later, Beatrix Potter informed Norman Warne that she

Beatrix with Benjamin Bouncer on a lead in 1891

was making good progress with the drawings, and on 27th August she wrote, 'I have drawn a good many sketches for backgrounds of rabbits already which is perhaps as well, as the rain has come here at last.' By the end of the summer the backgrounds for *The Tale of Benjamin Bunny* were completed. Back in London Beatrix settled down for the winter months to continue working on the new book. In the middle of February 1904 Beatrix Potter wrote to Warne, 'I have nearly finished B. Bunny except the cat.'

Over the course of working together, Beatrix and her editor had established a warm rapport. Though Beatrix's visits to the Frederick Warne offices were always chaperoned, the two exchanged letters nearly every day which allowed their friendship to flourish. On 25th July 1905, Norman Warne sent Beatrix a proposal of marriage, which she immediately accepted despite her parents' disapproval. At 39 years of age, Beatrix was determined to follow her heart, though she did appease her parents by keeping the engagement a secret. Unfortunately, only one month later, Norman died suddenly from a form of leukemia while Beatrix was on holiday with her family. Devastated, Beatrix took solace in her work. Earlier that summer Beatrix had used her book royalties to purchase Hill Top Farm, a working farm in the Lake District village of Near Sawrey. She drew inspiration from the tranquil surrounding landscape and set to work on her next books.

In the early months of 1909 Beatrix put the finishing touches to a new story about Peter Rabbit and Benjamin Bunny. 'I have done lots of sketches—not all to the purpose—and will now endeavour to finish up the F. Bunnies without further delay.' *The Tale of The Flopsy Bunnies* is set in the garden of her uncle's house, Gwaynynog, in Wales, a charming old house in the middle of a rambling country garden which Beatrix loved to sketch. Always at her best when painting rabbits, flowers and gardens, Beatrix used her skills to great advantage when

Six pencil studies of Benjamin, drawn in 1890

Norman Warne

A preliminary watercolour drawing of the country gardens at Gwaynynog

Miniature letters from the Flopsy Bunnies, sent by Beatrix to a young reader

illustrating this little book. A number of her preliminary sketches for the garden scenes have survived and they show the care she took to prepare each illustration.

It was natural for Beatrix to invite her readers to find out what had happened to the grown-up Peter Rabbit and his naughty cousin. The villain of the tale is Mr. McGregor again, but Benjamin Bunny is now married to Peter Rabbit's sister, Flopsy, and the six Flopsy Bunnies of the title are their children. Beatrix recognised that her readers enjoyed the 'independence' of her characters. She understood that they liked to imagine Benjamin and Peter 'busily absorbed in their own doings' —even marrying and having a family—long after the story was over and the book was closed. Fond of the Flopsy Bunnies, Beatrix wrote about their adventures again as part of her collection of miniature letters for the children she knew. She wrote some tiny letters which appear to come from various little Flopsy bunnies. The letters decrease in size and content according to the age and size of each little brother and sister rabbit, until those supposedly written by the tiniest bunnies are nothing more than a scribble and a few kisses. Benjamin and Flopsy's large family, which they have great difficulty keeping track of, was the subject for another little book published in 1912. *The Tale of Mr. Tod* is about the kidnapping of the bunnies by an unpleasant badger named Tommy Brock. Tommy Brock brings the baby rabbits to the house of Mr. Tod, the fox, and very nearly eats them. Disaster is only averted when a terrific battle between Mr. Tod and his uninvited house guest distracts the two predators from the bunnies. Once again, Benjamin turns to his cousin Peter for assistance, and together they stage a daring rescue of the babies. Another of Peter's sisters, Cotton-tail, makes a brief appearance when she points the rescue party in the right direction.

A long, rather dark Tale featuring disagreeable principal characters, *The Tale of Mr. Tod* marked a change from writing what Beatrix described as, 'goody goody books about nice people'. Due to her preoccupation with her new farming career, Beatrix had less time for painting and therefore the majority of the book's illustrations are framed line drawings in the style of woodcuts. The watercolours included, however, feature real-life landscapes of Sawrey. Bull Banks, where Mr. Tod lives in summer, was a pasture on Castle Farm, which Beatrix bought in 1909. Mr. Tod is also depicted walking along the banks of Esthwaite Water, one of Beatrix's favourite Lakeland views.

Beatrix's watercolour painting of the banks of Esthwaite Water

Although Beatrix's publishers worried that the protagonists in *The Tale of Mr. Tod* were unlikeable, Beatrix knew that children enjoyed reading about misconduct. *The Story of A Fierce Bad Rabbit*, published in 1906, was written for her editor's daughter. This little girl had complained that Peter was too good a rabbit and that she wanted a story about a really naughty one. Intended for very young children, this simple story was first published as a panorama, unfolding in a long strip of pictures and text from a wallet with a tuck-in flap. This format proved unpopular with booksellers, as the picture strips tended to get unrolled, and the story was reprinted in book form in 1916.

A first edition copy of The Story of A Fierce Bad Rabbit, *in panorama format*

*Beatrix and William Heelis
on their wedding day,
15th October 1913*

Beatrix used the same model for
The Tale of Tom Kitten *and*
The Story of Miss Moppet.

A year after the publication of *The Tale of Mr. Tod*, Beatrix married William Heelis at the age of 47. Settling permanently in the Lake District with her solicitor husband, Beatrix became increasingly engrossed in her second career as a farmer.

Hill Top Farm, Beatrix's Lake District home, provided Beatrix with the material for the next five stories in this treasury, all of which are set in and around Hill Top Farm and the village of Sawrey. She wrote about her property, 'It is indeed a funny old house and it would amuse children very much.'

Published in 1907, *The Tale of Tom Kitten* is about three misbehaved kittens who spoil their mother's dignified tea party. Any child who has ever been dressed in uncomfortable formal clothes will revel in Tom's mischief! *The Tale of Tom Kitten* is clearly set in Hill Top farmhouse and garden. Mrs. Tabitha Twitchit leads the disobedient kittens indoors through Hill Top's wicket gate, along the pretty garden path and up the house's staircase. Visitors standing on the porch, just as Mrs. Tabitha Twitchit does in the little book, can see the same view across rolling green fields. Beatrix Potter started work on the story in the summer of 1906, while she was in the middle of planning a traditional, unkempt garden at Hill Top. Because the garden at Hill Top has been so carefully preserved, many of the garden scenes in the book can still be identified there today.

Despite the strong association of the Twitchit family with Hill Top, when Beatrix began sketching *The Tale of Tom Kitten* she did not have a pet cat, and had to borrow one. The kitten proved to be a difficult model—adventurous and mischievous—rather like Tom Kitten himself. On 18th July 1906, she wrote, '. . . I have borrowed a kitten and I am rather glad of the opportunity of working at the drawings. It is very young and pretty and a most fearful pickle.' Although she found the kitten an exasperating model, Beatrix dedicated the Tale to 'all Pickles—

especially to those that get upon my garden wall'. Beatrix found ducks easier models than lively kittens. The clothes shed by the kittens in *The Tale of Tom Kitten* are discovered by the Puddle-duck family, who dress themselves in the discarded pinafores and tuckers. While visiting a cousin in London, Beatrix sketched the ducks in Putney Park. Jemima Puddle-duck, a determined but naive character, was the central character in Beatrix's next book, published in 1908.

Set in Hill Top farmyard, *The Tale of Jemima Puddle-Duck* was based on real life events. Jemima was one of the farm ducks who was always wandering off to lay her

Beatrix Potter on Hill Top porch, 1913

eggs. The tenant farmer's wife, Mrs. Cannon, had to sometimes substitute a hen to sit on Jemima's neglected eggs. The Cannon family actually appears in the book: we see Mrs. Cannon feeding the poultry, and in another picture her son Ralph looks for eggs among the rhubarb while her daughter, Betsy, passes beyond the gate. This blend of fantasy and reality lends a ring of truth to Beatrix's imaginary world.

Many of Beatrix's real-life animals feature in the Tale. Kep, who rescues Jemima from the fox, was Beatrix's devoted and loyal working sheepdog. Beatrix's Herdwick sheep, a breed native to the Lake District, can be seen in the background, as well as the farm's chickens, horses and cows.

Beatrix enjoyed sketching her farmyard animals, such as these ducks and hen, and closely observed their behaviour.

Observing her farm animals clearly gave Beatrix a lot of pleasure, and she often wrote about them with great affection. 'I seem to be able to tame any sort of animal,' she wrote in a letter, 'it is sometimes rather awkward on a farm, we cannot keep them out of the house, especially the Puddleducks, and turkeys.'

The Tale of Jemima Puddle-Duck is so closely associated with Hill Top Farm that it has been described as 'a poem about the farm itself'. The pictures in the story closely resemble views of Hill Top and the idyllic landscapes surrounding the farm are still recognisable today. The background view, in which Jemima sets off to look for a secret nesting place, can be seen from the far end of the farmyard. The ornamental ironwork gate which leads into a small vegetable garden still exists. In the little village of Near Sawrey, the entrance to the Tower Bank Arms looks very much as it did when Beatrix painted it.

When she bought Hill Top Farm Beatrix Potter decided not to alter the insides at all, and made no modern additions that might change the tone of it. She used it as her studio and study, keeping her precious drawings there. One problem facing Beatrix when she moved to Hill Top was an infestation of rats. In a letter to a friend she wrote, 'It really is delightful—if the rats could be stopped out!' Her battle to exterminate the farmhouse rodents, which could be heard overhead scuttering under the floorboards, inspired a story written in 1906. Beatrix always maintained a sense of humour about the rats and dedicated the new book to an intelligent pet rat named Sammy that she had once kept as a pet.

The Tale of Samuel Whiskers continues the adventures of the irrepressible Tom Kitten. Tom climbs up the chimney to hide from his mother and falls into the clutches of an enormous rat named Samuel Whiskers and his subservient wife, Anna Maria. After binding poor Tom, the rats attempt to bake him into a dumpling roly-poly pudding. Fortunately, their plan is thwarted by Tabitha Twitchit and Cousin Ribby, who rescue the errant kitten just in time. Originally called *The Roly-Poly Pudding*, the Tale was first published in 1908 in a large format which allowed Beatrix to include black and white drawings. The story is set in the Twitchit family residence, and thus the illustrations depict the farmhouse: the old-fashioned kitchen range that Tom climbs up, the staircase descended by a frantic Tabitha Twitchit, the dresser that Anna Maria scurries past and the front door through which Cousin Ribby appears are all detailed studies of Hill Top's interior. The scenic landscape seen from the chimney top is a view of Near Sawrey from Hill Top's roof. Beatrix even painted herself in the story, watching the rats running away from the farmhouse with their wheelbarrow of pilfered goods.

Visitors in Near Sawrey can still have a drink at the Tower Bank Arms.

Beatrix used her pet rat, Samuel Whiskers, as her model for this early fantasy picture.

The peculiar DREAM of Mr Samuel Whiskers, upon the subject of DUTCH CHEESE

A view of 5 Hill Top featured in The Tale of Tom Kitten.

A background sketch of the larder at Lakefield Cottage, drawn in 1902

Cousin Ribby is the heroine of the ninth Tale in this collection. Published in 1905, *The Tale of The Pie and The Patty-Pan* was the first story Beatrix set in Near Sawrey and is the only book to mention the village by name. When she hears that Cousin Ribby has invited Duchess to tea, an indignant Tabitha Twitchit exclaims, 'A little dog indeed! Just as if there were no CATS in Sawrey!' The tea party results in a series of very amusing misunderstandings stemming from the veal and ham pie which Duchess substitutes for Ribby's mouse pie.

The character of Duchess was based on two Pomeranian dogs belonging to Mrs. Rogerson, the wife of the gardener at Lakefield Cottage. On her third holiday in Sawrey in 1902, Beatrix stayed at Lakefield Cottage and sketched the interior, which became the background for Ribby's home. Duchess lives at Buckle Yeat, which was then the Near Sawrey Post Office, and the illustration where Duchess

reads the invitation shows the Buckle Yeat garden overspilling with poppies and snapdragons. The frontispiece illustration features Hill Top in the background as Ribby crosses the meadow carrying butter and milk.

This background painting of Buckle Yeat garden is nearly identical to the illustration in The Tale of The Pie and The Patty-Pan.

Duchess lives opposite the village shop that provided the setting for a story published in 1909. *The Tale of Ginger and Pickles* is about a tom-cat and terrier who run a village store. To the dismay of their customers, they are bankrupted by giving unlimited credit and close the shop. Dedicated to the owner of the village shop in Near Sawrey, the story proved popular with the villagers and Beatrix described their reaction in a letter to a friend. 'The "Ginger & Pickle" book has been causing much amusement, it has got a good many views which

*A preliminary watercolour of the
'Ginger and Pickles' shop interior*

*Troutbeck Park Farm, purchased
in 1924, was one of the many farms
that Beatrix bequeathed to the
National Trust.*

can be recognised in the village which is what they like, they are all quite jealous of each others houses & cats getting into a book.'

Originally published in a large format, the bigger size enabled Beatrix to depict the shop interior in detail. The story features familiar friends from previous books. Tom Kitten, Mittens and Moppet peer through the shop window in the frontispiece. Samuel Whiskers, who has run up a long bill for bacon and snuff, waits at the counter. The shopkeepers suspect Anna Maria of stealing cream crackers and Jemima Puddle-duck is pictured shopping with her ducklings. *The Tale of Ginger and Pickles*, a celebration of Sawrey, unites both Beatrix's fictional and real-life village.

In 1909 Beatrix purchased Castle Farm, with fields adjoining Hill Top. Visitors to the Lake District admire its rolling landscapes and traditional farmhouses, but the area famous for its unspoilt beauty might look very different today but for Beatrix Potter's foresight. She felt a great need to keep her beloved Lake District preserved for future generations, and dedicated the last 30 years of her life to ensuring that the area remained untouched by developers. A practical businesswoman, Beatrix efficiently managed some estates for the National Trust.

Today, *The Tale of Peter Rabbit* has been translated into over 35 languages and is published all over the world. Timeless classics, the books continue to sell in their millions and have been treasured by generations of children. Peter can be found on products ranging from baby clothes to chocolates. This merchandising began with Beatrix Potter's own interest in finding new ways to explore and expand the imaginary world she had created. Enjoying business negotiations, Beatrix was actively involved in developing what she called her 'sideshows'. Beatrix always took care to ensure that the reproduction of her

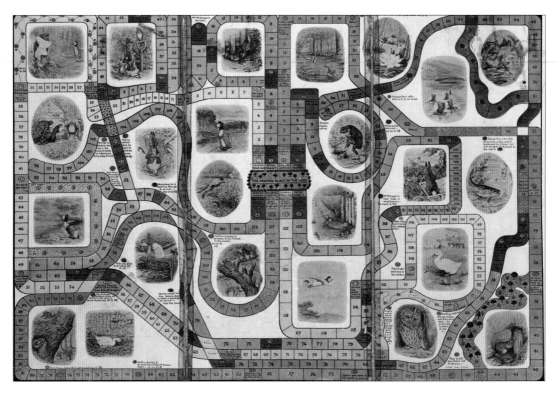

Peter Rabbit's Race Game, based on a 1907 design by Beatrix, was published in 1917.

characters on merchandise—whether on china tea sets, wooden figurines, games, dolls or painting books—was faithful to the original and retained the magic of the very first little 'rabbit book'. Towards the end of her life Beatrix Potter wrote, 'If I have done anything—even a little—to help small children on the road to enjoy and appreciate honest, simple pleasures, I have done a bit of good.'

When she died, Beatrix Potter left 4,000 acres of land to the nation. She dearly loved the countryside, and in her seventies she wrote, '. . . as I lie in bed, I can walk step by step on the fells and rough lands, seeing every stone and flower . . . where my old legs will never take me again.'

Beatrix Potter was a remarkable woman, with a truly orginal imagination, artistic and literary talent, and vision and the strength of mind to find creative fulfilment and financial independence.

Early Peter Rabbit merchandise

THE TALE OF
PETER RABBIT

TM

ABOUT THIS BOOK

The story of naughty Peter Rabbit in Mr. McGregor's garden first appeared in a picture letter Beatrix Potter wrote to Noel Moore, the young son of her former governess, in 1893. Encouraged by her success in having some greetings card designs published, Beatrix remembered the letter seven years later, and expanded it into a little picture book, with black-and-white illustrations. It was rejected by several publishers, so Beatrix had it printed herself, to give to family and friends.

About this time, Frederick Warne agreed to publish the tale if the author would supply colour pictures, and the book finally appeared in 1902, priced at one shilling (5p). It was an instant success, and has remained so ever since. It has a pacy story with an engaging hero, an exciting chase and a happy ending, matched with exquisite illustrations, and the result is a children's classic whose appeal is ageless.

ONCE UPON A TIME there were four little Rabbits, and their names were —

        Flopsy,
      Mopsy,
    Cotton-tail,
  and Peter.

They lived with their Mother in a sand-bank, underneath the root of a very big fir-tree.

"Now, my dears," said old Mrs. Rabbit one morning, "you may go into the fields or down the lane, but don't go into Mr. McGregor's garden.

"Your Father had an accident there; he was put in a pie by Mrs. McGregor.

"Now run along, and don't get into mischief. I am going out."

Then old Mrs. Rabbit took a basket and her umbrella, and went through the wood to the baker's. She bought a loaf of brown bread and five currant buns.

Flopsy, Mopsy and Cotton-tail, who were good little bunnies, went down the lane to gather blackberries;

But Peter, who was very
naughty, ran straight away
to Mr. McGregor's garden,

And squeezed under the gate!

First he ate some lettuces
and some French beans; and
then he ate some radishes;

And then, feeling rather
sick, he went to look
for some parsley.

But round the end of a cucumber
frame, whom should he meet
but Mr. McGregor!

Mr. McGregor was on his hands
and knees planting out young
cabbages, but he jumped up and
ran after Peter, waving a rake
and calling out, "Stop thief!"

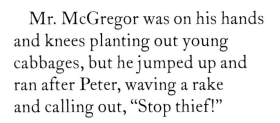

Peter was most dreadfully frightened; he rushed all over the garden, for he had forgotten the way back to the gate. He lost one of his shoes among the cabbages,

And the other shoe amongst the potatoes.

After losing them, he ran on four legs and went faster, so that I think he might have got away altogether if he had not unfortunately run into a gooseberry net, and got caught by the large buttons on his jacket. It was a blue jacket with brass buttons, quite new.

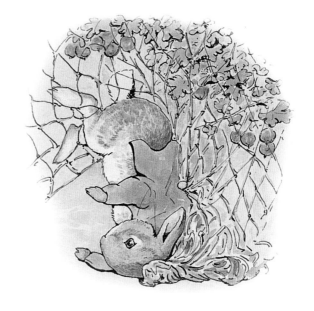

Peter gave himself up for lost, and shed big tears; but his sobs were overheard by some friendly sparrows, who flew to him in great excitement, and implored him to exert himself.

Mr. McGregor came up with a sieve, which he intended to pop upon the top of Peter; but Peter wriggled out just in time, leaving his jacket behind him,

And rushed into the tool-shed, and jumped into a can. It would have been a beautiful thing to hide in, if it had not had so much water in it.

Mr. McGregor was quite sure that Peter was somewhere in the tool-shed, perhaps hidden underneath a flower-pot. He began to turn them over carefully, looking under each. Presently Peter sneezed — "Kertyschoo!" Mr. McGregor was after him in no time,

And tried to put his foot upon Peter, who jumped out of a window, upsetting three plants. The window was too small for Mr. McGregor, and he was tired of running after Peter. He went back to his work.

Peter sat down to rest; he was out of breath and trembling with fright, and he had not the least idea which way to go. Also he was very damp with sitting in that can.

After a time he began to wander about, going lippity — lippity — not very fast, and looking all round.

He found a door in a wall; but it was locked, and there was no room for a fat little rabbit to squeeze underneath.

An old mouse was running in and out over the stone doorstep, carrying peas and beans to her family in the wood. Peter asked her the way to the gate, but she had such a large pea in her mouth that she could not answer. She only shook her head at him. Peter began to cry.

Then he tried to find his way straight across the garden, but he became more and more puzzled. Presently, he came to a pond where Mr. McGregor filled his watercans. A white cat was staring at some gold-fish; she sat very, very still, but now and then the tip of her tail twitched as if it were alive. Peter thought it best to go away without speaking to her; he had heard about cats from his cousin, little Benjamin Bunny.

He went back towards the
tool-shed, but suddenly, quite
close to him, he heard the noise
of a hoe — scr-r-ritch, scratch,
scratch, scritch. Peter scuttered
underneath the bushes.

But presently, as nothing happened,
he came out, and climbed upon
a wheelbarrow, and peeped over.
The first thing he saw was
Mr. McGregor hoeing onions.
His back was turned towards Peter,
and beyond him was the gate!

Peter got down very quietly
off the wheelbarrow, and started
running as fast as he could go,
along a straight walk behind
some black-currant bushes.
Mr. McGregor caught sight
of him at the corner, but Peter did
not care. He slipped underneath
the gate, and was safe at last in
the wood outside the garden.

Mr. McGregor hung up the little jacket and the shoes for a scarecrow to frighten the blackbirds.

Peter never stopped running or looked behind him till he got home to the big fir-tree.

He was so tired that he flopped down upon the nice soft sand on the floor of the rabbit-hole, and shut his eyes. His mother was busy cooking; she wondered what he had done with his clothes. It was the second little jacket and pair of shoes that Peter had lost in a fortnight!

I am sorry to say that Peter was not very well during the evening.

His mother put him to bed, and made some camomile tea; and she gave a dose of it to Peter! "One table-spoonful to be taken at bed-time."

But Flopsy, Mopsy, and Cotton-tail had bread and milk and blackberries for supper.

THE END

THE TALE OF

BENJAMIN BUNNY

ABOUT THIS BOOK

The real-life Benjamin Bunny was a tame rabbit of Beatrix Potter's, whom she sketched constantly, and whose exploits continually amused her. "He is an abject coward, but believes in bluster, could stare our old dog out of countenance, chase a cat that has turned tail." Although Benjamin had died by 1904, when this story was published, Beatrix may well have been thinking of him when she created Peter Rabbit's cousin, Benjamin. Little Benjamin is a very self-possessed animal, who makes himself quite at home in Mr. McGregor's garden.

Beatrix sketched background scenes for the tale while on holiday at Fawe Park, a house with a beautiful garden in the Lake District. The book is dedicated to "the children of Sawrey from Old Mr. Bunny". Beatrix was later to settle in the Lake District village of Sawrey, buying a small farm there in 1905.

ONE MORNING a little
rabbit sat on a bank
He pricked his ears and
listened to the trit-trot,
trit-trot of a pony.

A gig was coming along
the road; it was driven by
Mr. McGregor, and beside
him sat Mrs. McGregor
in her best bonnet.

As soon as they had
passed, little Benjamin
Bunny slid down into
the road, and set off —
with a hop, skip and a
jump — to call upon his
relations, who lived in
the wood at the back of
Mr. McGregor's garden.

That wood was full of rabbit-holes; and in the neatest sandiest hole of all, lived Benjamin's aunt and his cousins — Flopsy, Mopsy, Cotton-tail and Peter.

Old Mrs. Rabbit was a widow; she earned her living by knitting rabbit-wool mittens and muffetees (I once bought a pair at a bazaar). She also sold herbs, and rosemary tea, and rabbit-tobacco (which is what *we* call lavender).

Little Benjamin did not very much want to see his Aunt.

He came round the back of the fir-tree, and nearly tumbled upon the top of his Cousin Peter.

Peter was sitting by himself. He looked poorly, and was dressed in a red cotton pocket-handkerchief.

"Peter," — said little Benjamin, in a whisper —
"who has got your clothes?"

Peter replied — "The scarecrow in Mr. McGregor's garden," and described how he had been chased about the garden, and had dropped his shoes and coat.

Little Benjamin sat down beside his cousin, and assured him that Mr. McGregor had gone out in a gig, and Mrs. McGregor also; and certainly for the day, because she was wearing her best bonnet.

Peter said he hoped that it would rain.

At this point, old Mrs. Rabbit's voice was heard inside the rabbit-hole, calling — "Cotton-tail! Cotton-tail! fetch some more camomile!"

Peter said he thought he might feel better if he went for a walk.

They went away hand
in hand, and got upon
the flat top of the wall at
the bottom of the wood.
From here they looked down
into Mr. McGregor's garden.
Peter's coat and shoes were
plainly to be seen upon the
scarecrow, topped with an
old tam-o-shanter of
Mr. McGregor's.

Little Benjamin said,
"It spoils people's clothes
to squeeze under a gate;
the proper way to get in, is
to climb down a pear tree."

Peter fell down head
first; but it was of no
consequence, as the
bed below was newly
raked and quite soft.

It had been sown
with lettuces.

They left a great many odd little foot-marks all over the bed, especially little Benjamin, who was wearing clogs.

Little Benjamin said that the first thing to be done was to get back Peter's clothes, in order that they might be able to use the pocket-handkerchief.

They took them off the scarecrow. There had been rain during the night; there was water in the shoes, and the coat was somewhat shrunk.

Benjamin tried on the tam-o-shanter, but it was too big for him.

Then he suggested that
they should fill the
pocket-handkerchief
with onions, as a little
present for his Aunt.

Peter did not seem
to be enjoying himself;
he kept hearing noises.

Benjamin, on the contrary,
was perfectly at home,
and ate a lettuce leaf.
He said that he was in
the habit of coming to
the garden with his
father to get lettuces
for their Sunday dinner.

(The name of little
Benjamin's papa was old
Mr. Benjamin Bunny.)

The lettuces certainly
were very fine.

Peter did not eat anything; he said he should like to go home. Presently he dropped half the onions.

Little Benjamin said that it was not possible to get back up the pear tree, with a load of vegetables. He led the way boldly towards the other end of the garden. They went along a little walk on planks, under a sunny red-brick wall.

The mice sat on their door-steps cracking cherry-stones; they winked at Peter Rabbit and little Benjamin Bunny.

Presently Peter let
the pocket-handkerchief
go again.

They got amongst
flower-pots, and frames
and tubs; Peter heard
noises worse than ever,
his eyes were as big as
lolly-pops!

He was a step or two in
front of his cousin, when
he suddenly stopped.

This is what those little rabbits saw round that corner!

Little Benjamin took one look, and then, in half a minute less than no time, he hid himself and Peter and the onions underneath a large basket . . .

The cat got up and stretched herself, and came and sniffed at the basket.

Perhaps she liked the smell of onions!

Anyway, she sat down upon the top of the basket.

She sat there for *five hours*.

*

I cannot draw you a picture
of Peter and Benjamin
underneath the basket,
because it was quite dark,
and because the smell of
onions was fearful; it made
Peter Rabbit and little
Benjamin cry.

The sun got round behind the wood, and it was quite late in the
afternoon; but still the cat sat upon the basket.

At length there was a
pitter-patter, pitter-patter,
and some bits of mortar
fell from the wall above.

The cat looked up and
saw old Mr. Benjamin
Bunny prancing along
the top of the wall of
the upper terrace.

He was smoking a pipe
of rabbit-tobacco, and had
a little switch in his hand.

He was looking for his son.

Old Mr. Bunny had no opinion whatever of cats.

He took a tremendous jump off the top of the wall on to the top of the cat, and cuffed it off the basket, and kicked it into the green-house, scratching off a handful of fur.

The cat was too much surprised to scratch back.

When old Mr. Bunny had driven the cat into the green-house, he locked the door.

Then he came back to the basket and took out his son Benjamin by the ears, and whipped him with the little switch.

Then he took out his nephew Peter.

Then he took out
the handkerchief of
onions, and marched
out of the garden.

When Mr. McGregor
returned about half an hour
later, he observed several
things which perplexed him.

It looked as though some
person had been walking all
over the garden in a pair of
clogs —only the foot-marks
were too ridiculously little!

Also he could not
understand how the cat
could have managed to
shut herself up *inside* the
green-house, locking
the door upon the *outside*.

When Peter got home, his mother forgave him, because she was so glad to see that he had found his shoes and coat. Cotton-tail and Peter folded up the pocket-handkerchief, and old Mrs. Rabbit strung up the onions and hung them from the kitchen ceiling, with the bunches of herbs and the rabbit-tobacco.

THE END

THE TALE OF
THE FLOPSY BUNNIES

ABOUT THIS BOOK

The Tale of The Flopsy Bunnies pays another visit to the world of Peter Rabbit and Benjamin Bunny. Both rabbits have now grown up, Benjamin has married Peter's sister Flopsy and although still "improvident and cheerful", has a large family to care for. Beatrix Potter was well aware that her earlier books had created a huge demand for rabbit stories, and dedicated this one, "For all little friends of Mr. McGregor and Peter and Benjamin." Besides, she enjoyed painting rabbits, and gardens too. When preparing the book in 1909 she was staying with her uncle Fred and aunt Harriet Burton at Gwaynynog, their large house in Wales, and made many studies of the garden there. She described it on an earlier visit as "the prettiest kind of garden, where bright old-fashioned flowers grow amongst the currant bushes". It is beautifully depicted in her lovely illustrations.

IT IS SAID that the effect of eating too much lettuce is "soporific".

I have never felt sleepy after eating lettuces; but then *I* am not a rabbit.

They certainly had a very soporific effect upon the Flopsy Bunnies!

When Benjamin Bunny grew up, he married his Cousin Flopsy. They had a large family, and they were very improvident and cheerful.

I do not remember the separate names of their children; they were generally called the "Flopsy Bunnies".

As there was not always quite enough to eat — Benjamin used to borrow cabbages from Flopsy's brother, Peter Rabbit, who kept a nursery garden.

Sometimes Peter Rabbit had no cabbages to spare.

When this happened, the Flopsy Bunnies went across the field to a rubbish heap, in the ditch outside Mr. McGregor's garden.

Mr. McGregor's rubbish heap was a mixture. There were jam pots and paper bags, and mountains of chopped grass from the mowing machine (which always tasted oily), and some rotten vegetable marrows and an old boot or two. One day — oh joy! — there were a quantity of overgrown lettuces, which had "shot" into flower.

The Flopsy Bunnies simply stuffed lettuces. By degrees, one after another, they were overcome with slumber, and lay down in the mown grass.

Benjamin was not so much overcome as his children. Before going to sleep he was sufficiently wide awake to put a paper bag over his head to keep off the flies.

The little Flopsy Bunnies slept delightfully in the warm sun. From the lawn beyond the garden came the distant clacketty sound of the mowing machine. The bluebottles buzzed about the wall, and a little old mouse picked over the rubbish among the jam pots.

(I can tell you her name, she was called Thomasina Tittlemouse, a wood-mouse with a long tail.)

She rustled across the paper bag, and awakened Benjamin Bunny.

The mouse apologized profusely, and said that she knew Peter Rabbit.

While she and Benjamin were talking, close under the wall, they heard a heavy tread above their heads; and suddenly Mr. McGregor emptied out a sackful of lawn mowings right upon the top of the sleeping Flopsy Bunnies! Benjamin shrank down under his paper bag. The mouse hid in a jam pot.

The little rabbits smiled sweetly in their sleep under the shower of grass; they did not awake because the lettuces had been so soporific.

They dreamt that their mother Flopsy was tucking them up in a hay bed.

Mr. McGregor looked down after emptying his sack. He saw some funny little brown tips of ears sticking up through the lawn mowings. He stared at them for some time.

Presently a fly settled on one of them and it moved. Mr. McGregor climbed down on to the rubbish heap — "One, two, three, four! five! six leetle rabbits!" said he as he dropped them into his sack.

The Flopsy Bunnies dreamt that their mother was turning them over in bed. They stirred a little in their sleep, but still they did not wake up.

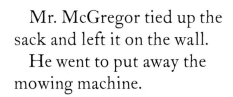

Mr. McGregor tied up the sack and left it on the wall. He went to put away the mowing machine.

While he was gone, Mrs. Flopsy Bunny (who had remained at home) came across the field.

She looked suspiciously at the sack and wondered where everybody was?

Then the mouse came out of her jam pot, and Benjamin took the paper bag off his head, and they told the doleful tale.

Benjamin and Flopsy were in despair, they could not undo the string.

But Mrs. Tittlemouse was a resourceful person. She nibbled a hole in the bottom corner of the sack.

The little rabbits were pulled out and pinched to wake them.

Their parents stuffed the empty sack with three rotten vegetable marrows, an old blacking-brush and two decayed turnips.

Then they all hid under a bush and watched for Mr. McGregor.

Mr. McGregor came back
and picked up the sack,
and carried it off.

He carried it hanging down,
as if it were rather heavy.

The Flopsy Bunnies
followed at a safe distance.

They watched him
go into his house.

And then they crept up
to the window to listen.

Mr. McGregor threw down
the sack on the stone floor in
a way that would have been
extremely painful to the Flopsy
Bunnies, if they had happened
to have been inside it.

They could hear him drag his chair on the flags, and chuckle —

"One, two, three, four, five, six leetle rabbits!" said Mr. McGregor.

"Eh? What's that? What have they been spoiling now?" enquired Mrs. McGregor.

"One, two, three, four, five, six leetle fat rabbits!" repeated Mr. McGregor, counting on his fingers — "one, two, three —"

"Don't you be silly; what do you mean, you silly old man?"

"In the sack! one, two, three, four, five, six!" replied Mr. McGregor.

(The youngest Flopsy Bunny got upon the window-sill.)

Mrs. McGregor took hold of the sack and felt it. She said she could feel six, but they must be *old* rabbits, because they were so hard and all different shapes.

"Not fit to eat; but the skins will do fine to line my old cloak."

"Line your old cloak?" shouted Mr. McGregor — "I shall sell them and buy myself baccy!"

"Rabbit tobacco! I shall skin them and cut off their heads."

Mrs. McGregor untied the sack and put her hand inside.

When she felt the vegetables she became very very angry.

She said that Mr. McGregor had "done it a purpose".

And Mr. McGregor was very angry too. One of the rotten marrows came flying through the kitchen window, and hit the youngest Flopsy Bunny.

It was rather hurt.

Then Benjamin and Flopsy thought that it was time to go home.

So Mr. McGregor did not get his tobacco, and Mrs. McGregor did not get her rabbit skins.

But next Christmas Thomasina Tittlemouse got a present of enough rabbit-wool to make herself a cloak and a hood, and a handsome muff and a pair of warm mittens.

THE END

THE TALE OF
MR. TOD

TM

ABOUT THIS BOOK

With the publication of this story Beatrix Potter claimed to be tired of writing "goody goody books about nice people". Her principal characters, Mr. Tod (the old Saxon name for a fox) and Tommy Brock (the country word for a badger), are indeed disagreeable, though their story has a happy ending. There are not many colour pictures in the book, for Beatrix had less time for painting. Instead, she included many black-and-white illustrations in the style of woodcuts. The tale is set in Sawrey; Bull Banks, where Mr. Tod had his winter earth, was a pasture on Castle Farm, and Esthwaite Water can also be seen in some of the pictures. *Mr. Tod* was dedicated to "Francis William of Ulva – someday!" He was the baby son of Beatrix's cousin, Caroline Hutton, who had married the Laird of Ulva.

I HAVE MADE MANY BOOKS about well-behaved people. Now, for a change, I am going to make a story about two disagreeable people, called Tommy Brock and Mr. Tod.

Nobody could call Mr. Tod "nice". The rabbits could not bear him; they could smell him half a mile off. He was of a wandering habit and he had foxy whiskers; they never knew where he would be next.

One day he was living in a stick-house in the coppice, causing terror to the family of old Mr. Benjamin Bouncer. Next day he moved into a pollard willow near the lake, frightening the wild ducks and the water rats.

In winter and early spring he might generally be found in an earth amongst the rocks at the top of Bull Banks, under Oatmeal Crag.

He had half a dozen houses, but he was seldom at home.

The houses were not always empty when Mr. Tod moved *out;* because sometimes Tommy Brock moved *in;* (without asking leave).

Tommy Brock was a short bristly fat waddling person with a grin; he grinned all over his face. He was not nice in his habits. He ate wasp nests and frogs and worms; and he waddled about by moonlight, digging things up.

His clothes were very dirty; and as he slept in the day-time, he always went to bed in his boots. And the bed which he went to bed in, was generally Mr. Tod's.

Now Tommy Brock did occasionally eat rabbit-pie; but it was only very little young ones occasionally, when other food was really scarce. He was friendly with old Mr. Bouncer; they agreed in disliking the wicked otters and Mr. Tod; they often talked over that painful subject.

Old Mr. Bouncer was stricken in years. He sat in the spring

sunshine outside the burrow, in a muffler; smoking a pipe of rabbit-tobacco.

He lived with his son Benjamin Bunny and his daughter-in-law Flopsy, who had a young family. Old Mr. Bouncer was in charge of the family that afternoon, because Benjamin and Flopsy had gone out.

The little rabbit babies were just old enough to open their blue eyes and kick. They lay in a fluffy bed of rabbit wool and hay, in a shallow burrow, separate from the main rabbit-hole. To tell the truth — old Mr. Bouncer had forgotten them.

He sat in the sun, and conversed cordially with Tommy Brock, who was passing through the wood with a sack and a little spud which he used for digging, and some mole traps. He complained bitterly about the scarcity of pheasants' eggs, and accused Mr. Tod of poaching them. And the otters had

cleared off all the frogs while he was asleep in winter — "I have not had a good square meal for a fortnight, I am living on pig-nuts. I shall have to turn vegetarian and eat my own tail!" said Tommy Brock.

It was not much of a joke, but it tickled old Mr. Bouncer; because Tommy Brock was so fat and stumpy and grinning.

So old Mr. Bouncer laughed; and pressed Tommy Brock to come inside, to taste a slice of seed-cake and "a glass of my daughter Flopsy's cowslip wine". Tommy Brock squeezed himself into the rabbit-hole with alacrity.

Then old Mr. Bouncer smoked another pipe, and gave Tommy  Brock a cabbage leaf cigar which was so very strong that it made Tommy Brock grin more than ever; and the smoke filled the burrow. Old Mr. Bouncer coughed and laughed; and Tommy Brock puffed and grinned.

And Mr. Bouncer laughed and coughed, and shut his eyes because of the cabbage smoke . . .

When Flopsy and Benjamin came back — old Mr. Bouncer woke up. Tommy Brock and all the young rabbit babies had disappeared!

Mr. Bouncer would not confess that he had admitted anybody into the rabbit-hole. But the smell of badger was undeniable; and there were round heavy footmarks in the sand. He was in disgrace; Flopsy wrung her ears, and slapped him.

Benjamin Bunny set off at once after Tommy Brock.

There was not much difficulty in tracking him; he had left his footmark and gone slowly up the winding footpath through the wood. Here he had rooted up the moss and wood sorrel. There he had dug quite a deep hole for dog darnel; and had set a mole trap. A little stream crossed the way. Benjamin skipped lightly over dry-foot; the badger's heavy steps showed plainly in the mud.

The path led to a part of the thicket where the trees had been cleared; there were leafy oak stumps, and a sea of blue hyacinths — but the smell that made Benjamin stop, was not the smell of flowers!

Mr. Tod's stick house was before him; and, for once, Mr. Tod was at home. There was not only a foxy flavour in proof of it — there was smoke coming out of the broken pail that served as a chimney.

Benjamin Bunny sat up, staring; his whiskers twitched. Inside the stick house somebody dropped a plate, and said something. Benjamin stamped his foot, and bolted.

He never stopped till he came to the other side of the wood. Apparently Tommy Brock had turned the same way. Upon the top of the wall, there were again the marks of badger; and some ravellings of a sack had caught on a briar.

Benjamin climbed over the wall, into a meadow. He found another mole trap newly set; he was still upon the track of Tommy Brock. It was getting late in the afternoon. Other rabbits were coming out to enjoy the evening air. One of them in a blue coat by himself, was busily hunting for dandelions —"Cousin Peter! Peter Rabbit, Peter Rabbit!" shouted Benjamin Bunny.

The blue-coated rabbit sat up with pricked ears —

"Whatever is the matter, Cousin Benjamin? Is it a cat? or John Stoat Ferret?"

"No, no, no! He's bagged my family — Tommy Brock — in a sack — have you seen him?"

"Tommy Brock? How many, Cousin Benjamin?"

"Seven, Cousin Peter, and all of them twins! Did he come this way? Please tell me quick!"

"Yes, yes; not ten minutes since . . . he said they were *caterpillars;* I did think they were kicking rather hard, for caterpillars."

"Which way? Which way has he gone, Cousin Peter?"

"He had a sack with something 'live in it; I watched him set a mole trap. Let me use my mind, Cousin Benjamin; tell me from the beginning." Benjamin did so.

"My Uncle Bouncer has displayed a lamentable want of discretion for his years," said Peter reflectively; "but there are two hopeful circumstances. Your family is alive and kicking; and Tommy Brock has had refreshment. He will probably go to sleep, and keep them for breakfast."

"Which way?"

"Cousin Benjamin, compose yourself. I know very well which way. Because Mr. Tod was at home in the stick house he has gone to

Mr. Tod's other house, at the top of Bull Banks. I partly know, because he offered to leave any message at Sister Cotton-tail's; he said he would be passing." (Cotton-tail had married a black rabbit, and gone to live on the hill.)

Peter hid his dandelions, and accompanied the afflicted parent, who was all of a twitter. They crossed several fields and began to climb the hill; the tracks of Tommy Brock were plainly to be seen. He seemed to have put down the sack every dozen yards, to rest.

"He must be very puffed; we are close behind him, by the scent. What a nasty person!" said Peter.

The sunshine was still warm and slanting on the hill pastures. Halfway up, Cotton-tail was sitting in her doorway, with four or five half-grown little rabbits playing about her; one black and the others brown.

Cotton-tail had seen Tommy Brock

passing in the distance. Asked whether her husband was at home she replied that Tommy Brock had rested twice while she watched him.

He had nodded, and pointed to the sack, and seemed doubled up with laughing — "Come away, Peter; he will be cooking them; come quicker!" said Benjamin Bunny.

They climbed up and up — "He was at home; I saw his black ears peeping out of the hole." "They live too near the rocks to quarrel with their neighbours. Come on, Cousin Benjamin!"

When they came near the wood at the top of Bull Banks, they went cautiously. The trees grew amongst heaped up rocks; and there, beneath a crag — Mr. Tod had made one of his homes. It was at the top of a steep bank; the rocks and bushes overhung it. The rabbits crept up carefully, listening and peeping.

This house was something between a cave, a prison, and a tumble-down pig-stye. There was a strong door, which was shut and locked.

The setting sun made the window panes glow like red flame; but the kitchen fire was not alight. It was neatly laid with dry sticks, as the rabbits could see, when they peeped through the window.

Benjamin sighed with relief.

But there were preparations upon the kitchen table which made him shudder. There was an immense empty pie-dish of blue willow pattern, and a large carving knife and fork, and a chopper.

At the other end of the table was a partly unfolded tablecloth, a plate, a tumbler, a knife and fork, salt-cellar, mustard and a chair —

in short, preparations for one person's supper.

No person was to be seen, and no young rabbits. The kitchen was empty and silent; the clock had run down. Peter and Benjamin flattened their noses against the window, and stared into the dusk.

Then they scrambled round the rocks to the other side of the house. It was damp and smelly, and overgrown with thorns and briars.

The rabbits shivered in their shoes.

"Oh my poor rabbit babies! What a dreadful place; I shall never see them again!" sighed Benjamin.

They crept up to the bedroom window. It was closed and bolted like the kitchen. But there were signs that this window had been recently open; the cobwebs were disturbed, and there were fresh dirty footmarks upon the window-sill.

The room inside was so dark, that at first they could make out nothing; but they could hear a noise — a slow deep regular snoring grunt. And as their eyes became accustomed to the darkness, they perceived that somebody was asleep on Mr. Tod's bed, curled up under the blanket — "He has gone to bed in his boots," whispered Peter.

Benjamin, who was all of a twitter, pulled Peter off the window sill.

Tommy Brock's snores continued, grunty and regular from Mr. Tod's bed. Nothing could be seen of the young family.

The sun had set; an owl began to hoot in the wood. There were many unpleasant things lying about, that had much better have been buried; rabbit bones and skulls, and chickens' legs and other horrors. It was a shocking place, and very dark.

They went back to the front of the house, and tried in every way to move the bolt of the kitchen window. They tried to push up a rusty nail between the window sashes; but it was of no use, especially without a light.

They sat side by side outside the window, whispering and listening.

In half an hour the moon rose over the wood. It shone full and clear and cold, upon the house amongst the rocks, and in at the kitchen window. But alas, no little rabbit babies were to be seen!

The moonbeams twinkled on the carving knife and the pie-dish, and made a path of brightness across the dirty floor.

The light showed a little door in a wall beside the kitchen fireplace — a little iron door belonging to a brick oven, of that old-fashioned sort that used to be heated with faggots of wood.

And presently at the same moment Peter and Benjamin noticed that whenever they shook the window — the little door opposite shook in answer. The young family were alive; shut up in the oven!

Benjamin was so excited that it was a mercy he did not awake Tommy Brock, whose snores continued solemnly in Mr. Tod's bed. But there really was not very much comfort in the discovery. They could not open the window; and although the young family was alive — the little rabbits were quite incapable of letting themselves out; they were not old enough to crawl.

After much whispering, Peter and Benjamin decided to dig a tunnel. They began to burrow a yard or two lower down the bank. They hoped that they might be able to work between the large stones under the house; the kitchen floor was so dirty that it was impossible to say whether it was made of earth or flags.

They dug and dug for hours. They could not tunnel straight on account of stones; but by the end of the night they were under the kitchen floor. Benjamin was on his back, scratching upwards. Peter's claws were worn down; he was outside the tunnel, shuffling sand away. He called out that it was morning — sunrise; and that the jays were making a noise down below in the woods.

Benjamin Bunny came out of the dark tunnel, shaking the sand from his ears; he cleaned his face with his paws. Every minute the sun shone warmer on the top of the hill. In the valley there was a sea of white mist, with golden tops of trees showing through.

Again from the fields down below in the mist there came the angry cry of a jay — followed by the sharp yelping bark of a fox!

Then those two rabbits lost their heads completely. They did the most foolish thing that they could have done. They rushed into their short new tunnel, and hid themselves at the top end of it, under Mr. Tod's kitchen floor.

Mr. Tod was coming up Bull Banks, and he was in the very worst of tempers. First he had been upset by breaking the plate. It was his own fault; but it was a china plate, the last of the dinner service that had belonged to his grandmother, old Vixen Tod. Then the midges had been very bad. And he had failed

to catch a hen pheasant on her nest; and it had contained only five eggs, two of them addled. Mr. Tod had had an unsatisfactory night.

As usual, when out of humour, he determined to move house. First he tried the pollard willow, but it was damp; and the otters had left a dead fish near it. Mr. Tod likes nobody's leavings but his own.

He made his way up the hill; his temper was not improved by noticing unmistakable marks of badger. No one else grubs up the moss so wantonly as Tommy Brock.

Mr. Tod slapped his stick upon the earth and fumed; he guessed

where Tommy Brock had gone to. He was further annoyed by the jay bird which followed him persistently. It flew from tree to tree and scolded, warning every rabbit within hearing that either a cat or a fox was coming up the plantation. Once when it flew screaming over his head — Mr. Tod snapped at it, and barked.

He approached his house very carefully, with a large rusty key. He sniffed and his whiskers bristled. The house was locked up, but Mr. Tod had his doubts whether it was empty. He turned the rusty key in the lock; the rabbits below could hear it. Mr. Tod opened the door cautiously and went in.

The sight that met Mr. Tod's eyes in Mr. Tod's kitchen made Mr. Tod furious. There was Mr. Tod's chair, and Mr. Tod's pie-dish, and his knife and fork and mustard and salt-cellar and his tablecloth that he had left folded up in the dresser — all set out for supper (or breakfast) — without doubt for that odious Tommy Brock.

There was a smell of fresh earth and dirty badger, which fortunately overpowered all smell of rabbit.

But what absorbed Mr. Tod's attention was a noise — a deep slow regular snoring grunting noise, coming from his own bed.

He peeped through the hinges of the half-open bedroom door. Then he turned and came out of the house

in a hurry. His whiskers bristled and his coat-collar stood on end with rage.

For the next twenty minutes Mr. Tod kept creeping cautiously into the house, and retreating hurriedly out again. By degrees he ventured further in — right into the bedroom. When he was outside the house, he scratched up the earth with fury. But when he was inside — he did not like the look of Tommy Brock's teeth.

He was lying on his back with his mouth open, grinning from ear to ear. He snored peacefully and regularly; but one eye was not perfectly shut.

Mr. Tod came in and out of the bedroom. Twice he brought in his walking-stick, and once he brought in the coal-scuttle. But he thought better of it, and took them away.

When he came back after removing the coal-scuttle, Tommy Brock was lying a little more sideways; but he seemed even sounder asleep. He was an incurably indolent person; he was not in the least afraid of Mr. Tod; he was simply too lazy and comfortable to move.

Mr. Tod came back yet again into the bedroom with a clothes line. He stood a minute watching Tommy Brock and listening attentively to the snores. They were very loud indeed, but seemed quite natural.

Mr. Tod turned his back towards the bed, and undid the window. It creaked; he turned round with a jump. Tommy Brock, who had opened one eye — shut it hastily. The snores continued.

Mr. Tod's proceedings were peculiar, and rather uneasy, (because the bed was between the window and the door of the bedroom).

He opened the window a little way, and pushed out the greater part of the clothes line on to the window-sill. The rest of the line, with a hook at the end, remained in his hand.

Tommy Brock snored conscientiously. Mr. Tod stood and looked at him for a minute; then he left the room again.

Tommy Brock opened both eyes, and looked at the rope and grinned. There was a noise outside the window. Tommy Brock shut his eyes in a hurry.

Mr. Tod had gone out at the front door, and round to the back of the house. On the way, he stumbled over the rabbit burrow. If he had had any idea who was inside it, he would have pulled them out quickly.

His foot went through the tunnel nearly upon the top of Peter Rabbit and Benjamin, but fortunately he thought that it was some more of Tommy Brock's work.

He took up the coil of line from the sill, listened for a moment, and then tied the rope to a tree.

Tommy Brock watched him with one eye, through the window. He was puzzled.

Mr. Tod fetched a large heavy pailful of water from the spring, and staggered with it through the kitchen into his bedroom.

Tommy Brock snored industriously, with rather a snort.

Mr. Tod put down the pail beside the bed, took up the end of rope with the hook — hesitated, and looked at Tommy Brock. The snores were almost apoplectic; but the grin was not quite so big.

Mr. Tod gingerly mounted a chair by the head of the bedstead.

His legs were dangerously near to Tommy Brock's teeth.

He reached up and put the end of rope, with the hook, over the head of the tester bed, where the curtains ought to hang.

(Mr. Tod's curtains were folded up, and put away, owing to the house being unoccupied. So was the counterpane. Tommy Brock was covered with a blanket only.) Mr. Tod standing on the unsteady chair looked down upon him attentively; he really was a first prize sound sleeper!

It seemed as though nothing would waken him — not even the flapping rope across the bed.

Mr. Tod descended safely from the chair, and endeavoured to get up again with the pail of water. He intended to hang it from the hook, dangling over the head of Tommy Brock, in order to make a sort of shower-bath, worked by a string, through the window.

But naturally being a thin-legged person (though vindictive and sandy whiskered) — he was quite unable to lift the heavy weight to the level of the hook and rope. He very nearly overbalanced himself.

The snores became more and more apoplectic. One of Tommy Brock's hind legs twitched under the blanket, but still he slept on peacefully.

Mr. Tod and the pail descended from the chair without accident. After considerable thought, he emptied the water into a wash-basin and jug. The empty pail was not too heavy for him; he slung it up wobbling over the head of Tommy Brock.

Surely there never was such a sleeper! Mr. Tod got up and down, down and up on the chair.

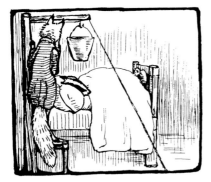

As he could not lift the whole pailful of water at once, he fetched a milk jug, and ladled quarts of water into the pail by degrees. The pail got fuller and fuller, and swung like a pendulum. Occasionally a drop splashed over; but still Tommy Brock snored regularly and never moved — except in one eye.

At last Mr. Tod's preparations were complete. The pail was full of water; the rope was tightly strained over the top of the bed, and across the window-sill to the tree outside.

"It will make a great mess in my bedroom; but I could never sleep

in that bed again without a spring-cleaning of some sort," said Mr. Tod. Mr. Tod took a last look at the badger and softly left the room. He went out of the house, shutting the front door. The rabbits heard his footsteps over the tunnel.

He ran round behind the house, intending to undo the rope in order to let fall the pailful of water upon Tommy Brock —

"I will wake him up with an unpleasant surprise," said Mr. Tod.

The moment he had gone, Tommy Brock got up in a hurry; he rolled Mr. Tod's dressing-gown into a bundle, put it into the bed beneath the pail of water instead of himself, and left the room also — grinning immensely.

He went into the kitchen, lighted the fire and boiled the kettle; for the moment he did not trouble himself to cook the baby rabbits.

When Mr. Tod got to the tree, he found that the weight and strain had dragged the knot so tight that it was past untying. He was obliged to gnaw it with his teeth. He chewed and gnawed for more than twenty minutes. At last the rope gave way with such a sudden jerk that it nearly pulled his teeth out, and quite knocked him over backwards.

Inside the house there was a great crash and splash, and the noise of a pail rolling over and over.

But no screams. Mr. Tod was mystified; he sat quite still, and listened attentively. Then he peeped in at the window. The water was dripping from the bed, the pail had rolled into a corner.

In the middle of the bed under the blanket, was a wet flattened *something* — much dinged in, in the middle where the pail had caught it (as it were across the tummy). Its head was covered by the wet blanket and it was *not snoring any longer*.

There was nothing stirring, and no sound except the drip, drop, drop drip of water trickling from the mattress.

Mr. Tod watched it for half an hour; his eyes glistened.

Then he cut a caper, and became so bold that he even tapped

at the window; but the bundle never moved.

Yes — there was no doubt about it — it had turned out even better than he had planned; the pail had hit poor old Tommy Brock, and killed him dead!

"I will bury that nasty person in the hole which he has dug. I will bring my bedding out, and dry it in the sun," said Mr. Tod.

"I will wash the tablecloth and spread it on the grass in the sun to bleach. And the blanket must be hung up in the wind; and the bed must be thoroughly disinfected, and aired with a warming-pan; and warmed with a hot-water bottle.

"I will get soft soap, and monkey soap, and all sorts of soap; and soda and scrubbing brushes; and persian powder; and carbolic to remove the smell. I must have a disinfecting. Perhaps I may have to burn sulphur."

He hurried round the house to get a shovel from the kitchen — "First I will arrange the hole — then I will drag out that person in the blanket..."

He opened the door...

Tommy Brock was sitting at Mr. Tod's kitchen table, pouring out tea from Mr. Tod's tea-pot into Mr. Tod's tea-cup. He was quite dry himself and grinning; and he threw the cup of scalding tea all over Mr. Tod.

Then Mr. Tod rushed upon Tommy Brock, and Tommy Brock grappled with Mr. Tod amongst the broken crockery, and there was

a terrific battle all over the kitchen. To the rabbits underneath it sounded as if the floor would give way at each crash of falling furniture.

They crept out of their tunnel, and hung about amongst the rocks and bushes, listening anxiously.

Inside the house the racket was fearful. The rabbit babies in the oven woke up trembling; perhaps it was fortunate they were shut up inside.

Everything was upset except the kitchen table.

And everything was broken, except the mantelpiece and the kitchen fender. The crockery was smashed to atoms.

The chairs were broken, and the window, and the clock fell with a crash,

and there were handfuls of Mr. Tod's sandy whiskers.

The vases fell off the mantelpiece, the canisters fell off the shelf; the kettle fell off the hob. Tommy Brock put his foot in a jar of raspberry jam.

And the boiling water out of the kettle fell upon the tail of Mr. Tod.

When the kettle fell, Tommy Brock, who was still grinning, happened to be uppermost; and he rolled Mr. Tod over and over like a log, out at the door.

Then the snarling and worrying went on outside; and they rolled over the bank, and down hill, bumping over the rocks.

There will never be any love lost between Tommy Brock and Mr. Tod.

As soon as the coast was clear, Peter Rabbit and Benjamin Bunny came out of the bushes —

"Now for it! Run in, Cousin Benjamin! Run in and get them! While I watch at the door."

But Benjamin was frightened —

"Oh; oh! they are coming back!"

"No they are not."

"Yes they are!"

"What dreadful bad language! I think they have fallen down the stone quarry."

Still Benjamin hesitated, and Peter kept pushing him —

"Be quick, it's all right. Shut the oven door, Cousin Benjamin, so that he won't miss them."

Decidedly there were lively doings in Mr. Tod's kitchen!

At home in the rabbit-hole, things had not been quite comfortable.

After quarrelling at supper, Flopsy and old Mr. Bouncer had passed a sleepless night, and quarrelled again at breakfast. Old Mr. Bouncer could no longer deny that he had invited company into the rabbit-hole; but he refused to reply to the questions and reproaches of Flopsy. The day passed heavily.

Old Mr. Bouncer, very sulky, was huddled up in a corner, barricaded with a chair. Flopsy had taken away his pipe and hidden the tobacco. She had been having a complete turn out and spring-cleaning, to relieve her feelings. She had just finished.

Old Mr. Bouncer, behind his chair, was wondering anxiously what she would do next.

In Mr. Tod's kitchen, amongst the wreckage, Benjamin Bunny picked his way to the oven nervously, through a thick cloud of dust. He opened the oven door, felt inside, and found something warm and wriggling. He lifted it out carefully, and rejoined Peter Rabbit.

"I've got them! Can we get away? Shall we hide, Cousin Peter?"

Peter pricked his ears; distant sounds of fighting still echoed in the wood.

Five minutes afterwards two breathless rabbits came scuttering away down Bull Banks, half carrying half dragging a sack between them, bumpetty bump over the grass. They reached home safely, and burst into the rabbit-hole.

Great was old Mr Bouncer's relief and Flopsy's joy when Peter and Benjamin arrived in triumph with the young family. The rabbit-babies were rather tumbled and very hungry; they were fed and put to bed. They soon recovered.

A long new pipe and a fresh supply of rabbit-tobacco was presented to Mr. Bouncer. He was rather upon his dignity; but he accepted.

Old Mr. Bouncer was forgiven, and they all had dinner. Then Peter and Benjamin told their story — but they had not waited long enough to be able to tell the end of the battle between Tommy Brock and Mr. Tod.

THE END

THE STORY OF
A FIERCE BAD RABBIT

™

ABOUT THIS BOOK

The Story of A Fierce Bad Rabbit, together with *The Story of Miss Moppet*, was first published as a panorama, unfolding in a long strip of pictures and text from a wallet with a tuck-in flap. Both books were intended for very young children; *The Story of A Fierce Bad Rabbit* had been written especially for editor Harold Warne's little daughter, Louie, who had told Beatrix that Peter was too good a rabbit, and she wanted a story about a *really* naughty one!

Unfortunately the panoramic format was not popular with the bookshops. As Beatrix wrote later: "The shops sensibly refused to stock them because they got unrolled and so bad to roll up again." In 1916, both stories were reprinted in book form and listed at the end of the series of Peter Rabbit books, alongside the nursery rhyme collections which were also intended for the very young.

THIS IS A FIERCE BAD RABBIT; look at his savage whiskers, and his claws and his turned-up tail.

This is a nice gentle Rabbit. His mother has given him a carrot.

The bad Rabbit
would like some carrot.

He doesn't say
"Please." He takes it!

And he scratches the
good Rabbit very badly.

The good Rabbit
creeps away, and hides
in a hole. It feels sad.

This is a man with a gun.

He sees something sitting on a bench. He thinks it is a very funny bird!

He comes creeping up behind the trees.

And then he shoots
— BANG!

This is what happens —

But this is all he finds on the bench, when he rushes up with his gun.

The good Rabbit peeps out of its hole,

And it sees the bad Rabbit tearing past — without any tail or whiskers!

THE END

THE TALE OF
TOM KITTEN

TM

ABOUT THIS BOOK

By the time Beatrix Potter started writing *The Tale of Tom Kitten*, she had owned Hill Top farm, in the Lake District village of Sawrey, for a year. The expansion of the farmhouse was finished, and Beatrix was enthusiastically planning her cottage garden. She could not completely desert her property for writing, and both house and garden feature in the story. Mrs. Tabitha Twitchit leads her children up the path to Hill Top's front door, while inside we see its staircase and bedrooms. The kittens romp through the garden's flowers to jump up on the wall overlooking Sawrey, and the ducks march across the farmyard.

Beatrix used the same kitten as a model for both Miss Moppet and Tom. "It is very young and pretty and a most fearful pickle." She dedicated this story to "all Pickles – especially to those that get upon my garden wall".

O NCE UPON A TIME
there were three little
kittens, and their names
were — Mittens, Tom Kitten,
and Moppet.

They had dear little fur
coats of their own; and they
tumbled about the doorstep
and played in the dust.

But one day their mother —
Mrs. Tabitha Twitchit —
expected friends to tea;
so she fetched the kittens
indoors, to wash and
dress them, before the
fine company arrived.

First she scrubbed their faces (this one is Moppet).

Then she brushed their fur (this one is Mittens).

Then she combed their tails and whiskers (this is Tom Kitten).

Tom was very naughty, and he scratched.

Mrs. Tabitha dressed Moppet and Mittens in clean pinafores and tuckers; and then she took all sorts of elegant uncomfortable clothes out of a chest of drawers, in order to dress up her son Thomas.

Tom Kitten was very fat, and he had grown; several buttons burst off. His mother sewed them on again.

When the three kittens were ready, Mrs. Tabitha unwisely turned them out into the garden, to be out of the way while she made hot buttered toast.

"Now keep your frocks clean, children! You must walk on your hind legs.

Keep away from the dirty ash-pit, and from Sally Henny-penny, and from the pig-stye and the Puddle-ducks."

Moppet and Mittens walked down the garden path unsteadily. Presently they trod upon their pinafores and fell on their noses. When they stood up there were several green smears!

"Let us climb up the rockery, and sit on the garden wall," said Moppet.

They turned their pinafores back to front, and went up with a skip and a jump; Moppet's white tucker fell down into the road.

Tom Kitten was quite unable to jump when walking upon his hind legs in trousers. He came up the rockery by degrees, breaking the ferns, and shedding buttons right and left.

He was all in pieces when he reached the top of the wall.

Moppet and Mittens tried to pull him together; his hat fell off, and the rest of his buttons burst.

While they were in difficulties, there was a pit pat paddle pat! and the three Puddle-ducks came along the hard high road, marching one behind the other and doing the goose step — pit pat paddle pat! pit pat waddle pat!

They stopped and stood in a row, and stared up at the kittens. They had very small eyes and looked surprised.

Then the two duck-birds, Rebeccah and Jemima Puddle-duck, picked up the hat and tucker and put them on.

Mittens laughed so that she fell off the wall. Moppet and Tom descended after her; the pinafores and all the rest of Tom's clothes came off on the way down.

"Come! Mr. Drake Puddle-duck," said Moppet — "Come and help us to dress him! Come and button up Tom!"

Mr. Drake Puddle-duck advanced in a slow sideways manner, and picked up the various articles.

But he put them on *himself!* They fitted him even worse than Tom Kitten.

"It's a very fine morning!" said Mr. Drake Puddle-duck.

And he and Jemima and Rebeccah Puddle-duck set off up the road, keeping step — pit pat, paddle pat! pit pat, waddle pat!

Then Tabitha Twitchit came down the garden and found her kittens on the wall with no clothes on.

She pulled them off the wall, smacked them, and took them back to the house.

"My friends will arrive in a minute, and you are not fit to be seen; I am affronted," said Mrs. Tabitha Twitchit.

She sent them upstairs; and I am sorry to say she told her friends that they were in bed with the measles; which was not true.

Quite the contrary; they were not in bed; *not* in the least.

Somehow there were very extraordinary noises over-head, which disturbed the dignity and repose of the tea-party.

And I think that some day I shall have to make another, larger, book, to tell you more about Tom Kitten!

As for the Puddle-ducks — they went into a pond. The clothes all came off directly, because there were no buttons.

And Mr. Drake Puddle-duck, and Jemima and Rebeccah, have been looking for them ever since.

THE END

THE TALE OF
JEMIMA
PUDDLE-DUCK

™

ABOUT THIS BOOK

Beatrix Potter's love of Hill Top and farming shine through this story. She painted her farm manager's wife, Mrs. Cannon, feeding the poulty, while the children Ralph and Betsy (to whom this "farmyard tale" is dedicated) are also illustrated. Kep the collie was Beatrix's favourite sheepdog, and Jemima herself was a real duck who lived at Hill Top. She is a most popular character: self-important, naive, but very endearing.

The story also contains many delightful views of Sawrey: Jemima's wood can still be seen, the view from the hills above the farm, across Esthwaite Water, has not changed, and the Tower Bank Arms is still the local village pub. This blend of fantasy and reality, so often to be found in Beatrix Potter's work, gives a ring of truth to her imaginary world.

WHAT A FUNNY SIGHT it is to see a brood of ducklings with a hen!
— Listen to the story of Jemima Puddle-duck, who was annoyed because the farmer's wife would not let her hatch her own eggs.

Her sister-in-law, Mrs. Rebeccah Puddle-duck, was perfectly willing to leave the hatching to some one else — "I have not the patience to sit on a nest for twenty-eight days; and no more have you, Jemima. You would let them go cold; you know you would!"

"I wish to hatch my own eggs; I will hatch them all by myself," quacked Jemima Puddle-duck.

She tried to hide her eggs; but they were always found and carried off.

Jemima Puddle-duck became quite desperate. She determined to make a nest right away from the farm.

She set off on a fine spring afternoon along the cart-road that leads over the hill.

She was wearing a shawl and a poke bonnet.

When she reached the top of the hill, she saw a wood in the distance.

She thought that it looked a safe quiet spot.

Jemima Puddle-duck was not much in the habit of flying. She ran downhill a few yards flapping her shawl, and then she jumped off into the air.

She flew beautifully when she had got a good start.

She skimmed along over the tree-tops until she saw an open place in the middle of the wood, where the trees and brushwood had been cleared.

Jemima alighted rather heavily, and began to waddle about in search of a convenient dry nesting-place.

She rather fancied a tree-stump amongst some tall fox-gloves.
But — seated upon the stump, she was startled to find an
elegantly dressed gentleman reading a newspaper. He had black prick
ears and sandy-coloured whiskers.

"Quack?" said Jemima Puddle-duck, with her head and her bonnet on one side — "Quack?"

The gentleman raised his eyes above his newspaper and looked curiously at Jemima —

"Madam, have you lost your way?" said he. He had a long bushy tail which he was sitting upon, as the stump was somewhat damp.

Jemima thought him mighty civil and handsome. She explained that
she had not lost her way, but
that she was trying to find a
convenient dry nesting-place.

"Ah! is that so? Indeed!"
said the gentleman with sandy
whiskers, looking curiously
at Jemima. He folded up the
newspaper, and put it in his
coat-tail pocket.

Jemima complained of the
superfluous hen.

"Indeed? How interesting!
I wish I could meet with
that fowl. I would teach it to
mind its own business!"

"But as to a nest — there is no difficulty: I have a sackful of feathers in my wood-shed. No, my dear madam, you will be in nobody's way. You may sit there as long as you like," said the bushy long-tailed gentleman.

He led the way to a very retired, dismal-looking house amongst the fox-gloves.

It was built of faggots and turf, and there were two broken pails, one on top of another, by way of a chimney.

"This is my summer residence; you would not find my earth — my winter house — so convenient," said the hospitable gentleman.

There was a tumble-down shed at the back of the house, made of old soap-boxes. The gentleman opened the door, and showed Jemima in.

The shed was almost quite full of feathers — it was almost suffocating; but it was comfortable and very soft.

Jemima Puddle-duck was rather surprised to find such a vast quantity of feathers. But it was very comfortable; and she made a nest without any trouble at all.

When she came out, the sandy-whiskered gentleman was sitting on a log reading the newspaper — at least he had it spread out, but he was looking over the top of it.

He was so polite, that he seemed almost sorry to let Jemima go home for the night. He promised to take great care of her nest until she came back again next day.

He said he loved eggs and ducklings; he should be proud to see a fine nestful in his wood-shed. Jemima Puddle-duck came every afternoon; she laid nine eggs in the nest. They were greeny white and very large. The foxy gentleman admired them immensely. He used

to turn them over and count them when Jemima was not there.

At last Jemima told him that she intended to begin to sit next day — "and I will bring a bag of corn with me, so that I need never leave my nest until the eggs are hatched. They might catch cold," said the conscientious Jemima.

"Madam, I beg you not to trouble yourself with a bag; I will provide oats. But before you commence your tedious sitting, I intend to give you a treat. Let us have a dinner-party all to ourselves! May I ask you to bring up some herbs from the farm-garden to make a savoury omelette? Sage and thyme, and mint and two onions, and some parsley. I will provide

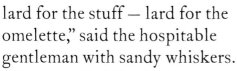

lard for the stuff — lard for the omelette," said the hospitable gentleman with sandy whiskers.

Jemima Puddle-duck was a simpleton: not even the mention of sage and onions made her suspicious. She went round the farm-garden, nibbling off snippets of all the different sorts of herbs that are used for stuffing roast duck.

129

And she waddled into the kitchen, and got two onions out of a basket.

The collie-dog Kep met her coming out. "What are you doing with those onions? Where do you go every afternoon by yourself, Jemima Puddle-duck?"

Jemima was rather in awe of the collie; she told him the whole story.

The collie listened, with his wise head on one side; he grinned when she described the polite gentleman with sandy whiskers.

He asked several questions about the wood, and about the exact position of the house and shed.

Then he went out, and trotted down the village. He went to look for two fox-hound puppies who were out at walk with the butcher.

Jemima Puddle-duck went
up the cart-road for the last
time, on a sunny afternoon.
She was rather burdened
with bunches of herbs and
two onions in a bag.

She flew over the wood, and alighted opposite the house of the
bushy long-tailed gentleman.

He was sitting on a log; he sniffed the air, and kept glancing
uneasily round the wood. When Jemima alighted he quite jumped.

"Come into the house
as soon as you have looked
at your eggs. Give me the
herbs for the omelette.
Be sharp!"

He was rather abrupt.
Jemima Puddle-duck
had never heard him
speak like that.

She felt surprised,
and uncomfortable.

While she was inside she
heard pattering feet round
the back of the shed. Some
one with a black nose
sniffed at the bottom of the
door, and then locked it.

Jemima became much
alarmed.

A moment afterwards
there were most awful
noises — barking, baying,
growls and howls,
squealing and groans.

And nothing more was ever seen
of that foxy-whiskered gentleman.

Presently Kep opened the
door of the shed, and let out
Jemima Puddle-duck.

Unfortunately the puppies
rushed in and gobbled up all the
eggs before he could stop them.

He had a bite on his ear and both the puppies were limping.
Jemima Puddle-duck was escorted home in tears on account of those eggs.

She laid some more in June, and she was permitted to keep them herself; but only four of them hatched.

Jemima Puddle-duck said that it was because of her nerves; but she had always been a bad sitter.

THE END

THE TALE OF

SAMUEL WHISKERS

OR THE ROLY-POLY PUDDING

ABOUT THIS BOOK

When this story was first published in 1908, it was entitled *The Roly-Poly Pudding*, and appeared in the larger size used for *The Pie and The Patty-Pan*. In 1926 it was reduced to the standard size and given the title we now know it by.

The tale was actually written in 1906, when Beatrix was exploring Hill Top, the farm she had recently bought. She described the house in a letter to a friend. "It really is delightful – if the rats could be stopped out! . . . I never saw such a place for hide and seek and funny cupboards and closets." Here was her inspiration for the further adventures of Tom Kitten: an old farmhouse, and her pet rat, to whom the book is dedicated, "In remembrance of Sammy, the intelligent pink-eyed representative of a persecuted (but irrepressible) race. An affectionate little friend and most accomplished thief."

ONCE UPON A TIME there was an old cat, called Mrs. Tabitha Twitchit, who was an anxious parent. She used to lose her kittens continually, and whenever they were lost they were always in mischief!

On baking day she determined to shut them up in a cupboard.

She caught Moppet and Mittens, but she could not find Tom.

Mrs. Tabitha went up and down all over the house, mewing for Tom Kitten. She looked in the pantry under the staircase, and she searched the best spare bedroom that was all covered up with dust sheets. She went right upstairs and looked into the attics, but she could not find him anywhere.

It was an old, old house, full of cupboards and passages. Some of the walls were four feet thick, and there used to be queer noises inside them, as if there might be a little secret staircase. Certainly there were odd little jagged doorways in the wainscot, and things disappeared at night — especially cheese and bacon.

Mrs. Tabitha became more and more distracted, and mewed dreadfully.

While their mother was searching the house, Moppet and Mittens had got into mischief.

The cupboard door was not locked, so they pushed it open and came out.

They went straight to the dough which was set to rise in a pan before the fire.

They patted it with their little soft paws — "Shall we make dear little muffins?" said Mittens to Moppet.

But just at that moment somebody knocked at the front door, and Moppet jumped into the flour barrel in a fright.

Mittens ran away to the dairy, and hid in an empty jar on the stone shelf where the milk pans stand.

The visitor was a neighbour, Mrs. Ribby; she had called to borrow some yeast.

Mrs. Tabitha came downstairs mewing dreadfully — "Come in, Cousin Ribby, come in, and sit ye down! I'm in sad trouble, Cousin Ribby," said Tabitha, shedding tears. "I've lost my dear son Thomas; I'm afraid the rats have got him." She wiped her eyes with her apron. "He's a bad kitten, Cousin Tabitha; he made a cat's cradle of my best bonnet last time I came to tea. Where have you looked for him?"

"All over the house!
The rats are too many for
me. What a thing it is to
have an unruly family!"
said Mrs. Tabitha Twitchit.

"I'm not afraid of rats;
I will help you to find him;
and whip him too! What is
all that soot in the fender?"

"The chimney wants sweeping — Oh, dear me, Cousin Ribby — now Moppet and Mittens are gone!

"They have both got out of the cupboard!"

Ribby and Tabitha set to work to search the house thoroughly again. They poked under the beds with Ribby's umbrella, and they rummaged in cupboards. They even fetched a candle, and looked inside a clothes chest in one of the attics. They could not find anything, but once they heard a door bang and somebody scuttered downstairs.

"Yes, it is infested with rats," said Tabitha tearfully. "I caught seven young ones out of one hole in the back kitchen, and we had them for dinner last Saturday. And once I saw the old father rat — an enormous old rat, Cousin Ribby. I was just going to jump upon him, when he showed his yellow teeth at me and whisked down the hole.

"The rats get upon my nerves, Cousin Ribby," said Tabitha.

Ribby and Tabitha searched and searched. They both heard a curious roly-poly noise under the attic floor. But there was nothing to be seen.

They returned to the kitchen. "Here's one of your kittens at least," said Ribby, dragging Moppet out of the flour barrel.

They shook the flour off her and set her down on the kitchen floor. She seemed to be in a terrible fright.

"Oh! Mother, Mother," said Moppet, "there's been an old woman rat in the kitchen, and she's stolen some of the dough!"

The two cats ran to look at the dough pan. Sure enough there were marks of little scratching fingers, and a lump of dough was gone!

"Which way did she go, Moppet?"

But Moppet had been too much frightened to peep out of the barrel again.

Ribby and Tabitha took her with them to keep her safely in sight, while they went on with their search.

They went into the dairy.

The first thing they found was Mittens, hiding in an empty jar.

They tipped up the jar, and she scrambled out.

"Oh, Mother, Mother!" said Mittens —

"Oh! Mother, Mother, there has been an old man rat in the dairy — a dreadful 'normous big rat, Mother; and he's stolen a pat of butter and the rolling-pin."

Ribby and Tabitha looked at one another.

"A rolling-pin and butter! Oh, my poor son Thomas!"

exclaimed Tabitha, wringing her paws.

"A rolling-pin?" said Ribby. "Did we not hear a roly-poly noise in the attic when we were looking into that chest?"

Ribby and Tabitha rushed upstairs again. Sure enough the roly-poly noise was still going on quite distinctly under the attic floor.

"This is serious, Cousin Tabitha," said Ribby. "We must send for John Joiner at once, with a saw."

*

Now this is what had been happening to Tom Kitten, and it shows how very unwise it is to go up a chimney in a very old house, where a person does not know his way, and where there are enormous rats.

Tom Kitten did not want to be shut up in a cupboard. When he saw that his mother was going to bake, he determined to hide.

He looked about for a nice convenient place, and he fixed upon the chimney.

The fire had only just been lighted, and it was not hot; but there was a white choky smoke from the green sticks. Tom Kitten got upon the fender and looked up. It was a big old-fashioned fire-place.

The chimney itself was wide enough inside for a man to stand up and walk about. So there was plenty of room for a little Tom Cat.

He jumped right up into the fire-place, balancing himself upon the iron bar where the kettle hangs.

Tom Kitten took another big jump off the bar, and landed on a ledge high up inside the chimney, knocking down some soot into the fender.

Tom Kitten coughed and choked with the smoke; and he could hear the sticks beginning to crackle and burn in the fire-place down below. He made up his mind to climb right to the top, and get out on the slates, and try to catch sparrows.

"I cannot go back. If I slipped I might fall in the fire and singe my beautiful tail and my little blue jacket."

The chimney was a very big old-fashioned one. It was built in the days when people burnt logs of wood upon the hearth.

The chimney stack stood up above the roof like a little stone tower, and the daylight shone down from the top, under the slanting slates that kept out the rain.

Tom Kitten was getting very frightened! He climbed up, and up, and up.

Then he waded sideways through inches of soot. He was like a little sweep himself.

It was most confusing in the dark. One flue seemed to lead into another. There was less smoke, but Tom Kitten felt quite lost.

He scrambled up and up; but before he reached the chimney top he came to a place where somebody had loosened a stone in the wall. There were some mutton bones lying about —

"This seems funny," said Tom Kitten. "Who has been gnawing bones up here in the chimney? I wish I had never come! And what a funny smell? It is something like mouse; only dreadfully strong. It makes me sneeze," said Tom Kitten.

He squeezed through the hole in the wall, and dragged himself along a most uncomfortably tight passage where there was scarcely any light.

He groped his way carefully for several yards; he was at the back of the skirting-board in the attic, where there is a little mark * in the picture.

All at once he fell head over heels in the dark, down a hole, and landed on a heap of very dirty rags.

When Tom Kitten picked himself up and looked about him — he found himself in a place that he had never seen before, although he had lived all his life in the house.

It was a very small stuffy fusty room, with boards, and rafters, and cobwebs, and lath and plaster.

Opposite to him — as far away as he could sit — was an enormous rat.

"What do you mean by tumbling into my

bed all covered with smuts?" said the rat, chattering his teeth.

"Please, sir, the chimney wants sweeping," said poor Tom Kitten. "Anna Maria! Anna Maria!" squeaked the rat. There was a pattering noise and an old woman rat poked her head round a rafter. All in a minute she rushed upon Tom Kitten, and before he knew what was happening —

His coat was pulled off, and he was rolled up in a bundle, and tied with string in very hard knots.

Anna Maria did the tying. The old rat watched her and took snuff. When she had finished, they both sat staring at him with their mouths open.

"Anna Maria," said the old man rat (whose name was Samuel Whiskers) — "Anna Maria, make me a kitten dumpling roly-poly pudding for my dinner."

"It requires dough and a pat of butter, and a rolling-pin," said Anna Maria, considering Tom Kitten with her head on one side.

"No," said Samuel Whiskers, "make it properly, Anna Maria, with breadcrumbs."

"Nonsense! Butter and dough," replied Anna Maria.

The two rats consulted together for a few minutes and then went away.

Samuel Whiskers got through a hole in the wainscot, and went boldly down the front staircase to the dairy to get the butter. He did not meet anybody.

He made a second journey for the rolling-pin. He pushed it in front of him with his paws, like a brewer's man trundling a barrel.

He could hear Ribby and Tabitha talking, but they were busy lighting the candle to look into the chest. They did not see him.

Anna Maria went down by way of the skirting-board and a window shutter to the kitchen to steal the dough.

She borrowed a small saucer, and scooped up the dough with her paws.

She did not observe Moppet.

While Tom Kitten was left alone under the floor of the attic, he wriggled about and tried to mew for help.

But his mouth was full of soot and cobwebs, and he was tied up in such very tight knots, he could not make anybody hear him.

Except a spider who came out of a crack in the ceiling and examined the knots critically, from a safe distance.

It was a judge of knots because it had a habit of tying up unfortunate blue-bottles. It did not offer to assist him.

Tom Kitten wriggled and squirmed until he was quite exhausted.

Then he nailed the plank down again, and put his tools in his bag, and came downstairs.

The cat family had quite recovered. They invited him to stay to dinner.

The dumpling had been peeled off Tom Kitten, and made separately into a bag pudding, with currants in it to hide the smuts.

They had been obliged to put Tom Kitten into a hot bath to get the butter off.

John Joiner smelt the pudding; but he regretted that he had not time to stay to dinner, because he had just finished making a wheelbarrow for Miss Potter, and she had ordered two hen-coops.

And when I was going to the post late in the afternoon — I looked up the lane from the corner, and I saw Mr. Samuel Whiskers and his wife on the run, with big bundles on a little wheelbarrow, which looked very like mine.

They were just turning in at the gate to the barn of Farmer Potatoes. Samuel Whiskers was puffing and out of breath. Anna Maria was still arguing in shrill tones.

She seemed to know her way, and she seemed to have a quantity of luggage.

I am sure *I* never gave her leave to borrow my wheelbarrow!

They went into the barn, and hauled their parcels with a bit of string to the top of the hay mow.

After that, there were no
more rats for a long time
at Tabitha Twitchit's.

As for Farmer Potatoes,
he has been driven nearly
distracted. There are rats,
and rats, and rats in his
barn! They eat up the
chicken food, and steal the
oats and bran, and make
holes in the meal bags.

And they are all
descended from Mr.
and Mrs. Samuel
Whiskers — children
and grand-children
and great great
grand-children.
 There is no end
to them!

Moppet and Mittens have grown up into very good rat-catchers.

They go out rat-catching in the village, and they find plenty of employment. They charge so much a dozen, and earn their living very comfortably.

They hang up the rats' tails in a row on the barn door, to show how many they have caught — dozens and dozens of them.

But Tom Kitten has always been afraid of a rat; he never durst face anything that is bigger than — A Mouse.

THE END

THE TALE OF
THE PIE AND THE
PATTY-PAN

™

ABOUT THIS BOOK

This story is rooted very firmly in the village of Sawrey, though Beatrix Potter was not yet living there when she sketched its lanes, houses and gardens in 1902. It was originally written in 1903, then laid aside until 1905. The tale reflects Beatrix's affection for the Lake District village and its inhabitants, and was one she was particularly pleased with: "If the book prints well it will be my next favourite to the *Tailor*." It was published in 1905, in a larger size than the other books, being reduced to the standard format in 1930 and then listed as the seventeenth of *The Original Peter Rabbit Books*. The dedication reads, "For Joan [one of the Moore daughters], to read to Baby" [Beatrix's god-daughter, named after her, born in November 1903].

ONCE UPON A TIME there was a Pussy-cat called Ribby, who invited a little dog called Duchess, to tea.

"Come in good time, my dear Duchess," said Ribby's letter, "and we will have something so very very nice. I am baking it in a pie-dish — a pie-dish with a pink rim. You never tasted anything so good! And *you* shall eat it all! *I* will eat muffins, my dear Duchess!" wrote Ribby.

Duchess read the letter and wrote an answer: "I will come with much pleasure at a quarter past four. But it is very strange. *I* was just going to invite you to come here, to supper, my dear Ribby, to eat something *most delicious*.

"I will come very punctually, my dear Ribby," wrote Duchess; and then at the end she added — "I hope it isn't mouse?"

And then she thought that did not look quite polite; so she scratched out "isn't mouse" and changed it to "I hope it will be fine," and she gave her letter to the postman.

But she thought a great deal about Ribby's pie, and she read Ribby's letter over and over again.

"I am dreadfully afraid it *will* be mouse!" said Duchess to herself— "I really couldn't, *couldn't* eat mouse pie. And I shall have to eat it, because it is a party. And *my* pie was going to be veal and ham. A pink and white pie-dish! and so is mine; just like Ribby's dishes; they were both bought at Tabitha Twitchit's."

Duchess went into her larder and took the pie off a shelf and looked at it.

"It is all ready to put into the oven. Such lovely pie-crust; and I put in a little tin patty-pan to hold up the crust; and I made a hole in the middle with a fork to let out the steam — Oh I do wish I could eat my own pie, instead of a pie made of mouse!"

Duchess considered and considered and read Ribby's letter again — "A pink and white pie-dish — and *you* shall eat it *all*. 'You' means me — then Ribby is not going to even taste the pie herself? A pink and white pie-dish! Ribby is sure to go out to buy the muffins . . . Oh what a good idea! Why shouldn't I rush along and put my pie into Ribby's oven when Ribby isn't there?"

Duchess was quite delighted with her own cleverness!

Ribby in the meantime had received Duchess's answer, and as soon as she was sure that the little dog could come — she popped *her* pie

into the oven. There were two ovens, one above the other; some other knobs and handles were only ornamental and not intended to open. Ribby put the pie into the lower oven; the door was very stiff.

"The top oven bakes too quickly," said Ribby to herself. "It is a pie of the most delicate and tender mouse minced up with bacon. And I have taken out all the bones; because Duchess did

nearly choke herself with a fish-bone last time I gave a party. She eats a little fast — rather big mouthfuls. But a most genteel and elegant little dog; infinitely superior company to Cousin Tabitha Twitchit."

Ribby put on some coal and swept up the hearth. Then she went out with a can to the well, for water to fill up the kettle.

Then she began to set the room in order, for it was the sitting-room as well as the kitchen. She shook the mats out at the front door and put them straight; the hearth-rug was a rabbit-skin. She dusted the clock and the ornaments on the mantelpiece, and she polished and rubbed the tables and chairs.

Then she spread a very clean white tablecloth, and set out her best china tea-set, which she took out of a wall-cupboard near the fire-place. The tea-cups

were white with a
pattern of pink roses;
and the dinner-plates
were white and blue.

When Ribby had
laid the table she took
a jug and a blue and
white dish, and went
out down the field
to the farm, to fetch
milk and butter.

When she came
back, she peeped into
the bottom oven; the
pie looked very
comfortable.

Ribby put on her
shawl and bonnet
and went out again
with a basket, to the

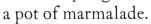

village shop to buy a packet of tea, a pound of lump sugar, and

a pot of marmalade.

And just at the same
time, Duchess came out
of *her* house, at the other
end of the village.

Ribby met Duchess half-
way down the street, also
carrying a basket, covered
with a cloth.

They only bowed to one

another; they did
not speak, because they
were going to have a party.

As soon as Duchess
had got round the corner
out of sight — she simply
ran! Straight away to
Ribby's house!

Ribby went into the shop and
bought what she required, and came out,
after a pleasant gossip with Cousin Tabitha Twitchit.

Cousin Tabitha was
disdainful afterwards
in conversation —
"A little *dog*
indeed! Just as if
there were no CATS
in Sawrey! And a
pie for afternoon
tea! The very idea!"
said Cousin Tabitha
Twitchit.

Ribby went on to
Timothy Baker's and
bought the muffins.
Then she went home.

There seemed to
be a sort of scuffling
noise in the back
passage, as she was
coming in at the
front door.

"I trust that is not that Pie; the spoons are locked up, however," said Ribby.

But there was nobody there. Ribby opened the bottom oven door with some difficulty, and turned the pie. There began to be a pleasing smell of baked mouse!

Duchess in the meantime, had slipped out at the back door.

"It is a very odd thing that Ribby's pie was *not* in the oven when I put mine in! And I can't find it anywhere; I have looked all over the house. I put *my* pie into a nice hot oven at the top. I could not turn any of the other handles; I think that they are all shams," said Duchess, "but I wish I could have removed the pie made of mouse! I cannot think what she has done with it? I heard Ribby coming and I had to run out by the back door!"

Duchess went home and brushed her beautiful black coat; and then she picked a bunch of flowers in her garden as a present for Ribby; and passed the time until the clock struck four.

Ribby — having assured herself by careful search that there was really no one hiding in the cupboard or in the larder — went upstairs to change her dress.

She put on a lilac silk gown, for the party, and an embroidered muslin apron and tippet.

"It is very strange," said Ribby, "I did not *think* I left that drawer pulled out; has somebody been trying on my mittens?"

She came downstairs again, and made the tea, and put the teapot on the hob. She peeped again into the *bottom* oven; the pie had become a lovely brown, and it was steaming hot.

She sat down before the fire to wait for the little dog. "I am glad I used the *bottom* oven," said Ribby, "the top one would certainly have been very much too hot. I wonder why that cupboard door was open? Can there really have been someone in the house?"

Very punctually at four o'clock, Duchess started to go to the party. She ran so fast through the village that she was too early, and she had to wait a little while in the lane that

leads down to
Ribby's house.

"I wonder if Ribby
has taken *my* pie out
of the oven yet?" said
Duchess, "and whatever
can have become of the
other pie made
of mouse?"

At a quarter past four
to the minute, there
came a most genteel
little tap-tappity. "Is
Mrs. Ribston at home?"
inquired Duchess
in the porch.

"Come in! and how
do you do? my dear
Duchess," cried Ribby.
"I hope I see you well?"

"Quite well, I

thank you, and how do *you* do, my dear Ribby?" said Duchess. "I've
brought you some flowers; what a delicious smell of pie!"

"Oh, what lovely flowers! Yes, it is mouse and bacon!"

"Do not talk about food, my dear Ribby," said Duchess; "what a
lovely white tea-cloth! . . . Is it done to a turn? Is it still in the oven?"

"I think it wants another five minutes," said Ribby. "Just a shade
longer; I will pour out the tea, while we wait. Do you take sugar,
my dear Duchess?"

"Oh yes, please! my dear Ribby; and may I have a lump
upon my nose?"

"With pleasure, my dear Duchess; how beautifully you beg! Oh, how sweetly pretty!"

Duchess sat up with the sugar on her nose and sniffed —

"How good that pie smells! I do love veal and ham — I mean to say mouse and bacon —"

She dropped the sugar in confusion, and had to go hunting under the tea-table, so she did not see which oven Ribby opened in order to get out the pie.

Ribby set the pie upon the table; there was a very savoury smell.

Duchess came out from under the tablecloth munching sugar, and sat up on a chair.

"I will first cut the pie for you; I am going to have muffin and marmalade," said Ribby.

"Do you really prefer muffin? Mind the patty-pan!"

"I beg your pardon?" said Ribby.

"May I pass you the marmalade?" said Duchess hurriedly.

The pie proved extremely toothsome, and the muffins light
and hot. They disappeared rapidly, especially the pie!

"I think" — (thought the Duchess to herself) — "I *think* it would
be wiser if I helped myself to pie; though Ribby did not seem to
notice anything when she was cutting it. What very small fine pieces
it has cooked into! I did not remember that I had minced it up so fine;
I suppose this is a quicker oven than my own."

"How fast Duchess is eating!" thought Ribby to herself, as she
buttered her fifth muffin.

The pie-dish was emptying rapidly!
Duchess had had four helps already,
and was fumbling with the spoon.

"A little more bacon, my dear Duchess?"
said Ribby.

"Thank you, my dear Ribby; I was only
feeling for the patty-pan."

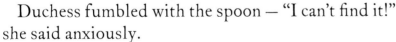

"The patty-pan? my dear Duchess?"

"The patty-pan that held up the pie-crust,"
said Duchess, blushing under her black coat.

"Oh, I didn't put one in, my dear Duchess,"
said Ribby; "I don't think that it is necessary
in pies made of mouse."

Duchess fumbled with the spoon — "I can't find it!"
she said anxiously.

"There isn't a patty-pan," said Ribby, looking perplexed.

"Yes, indeed, my dear Ribby; where can it have gone to?"
said Duchess.

"There most certainly is not one, my dear Duchess. I disapprove
of tin articles in puddings and pies. It is most undesirable —
(especially when people swallow in lumps!)" she added in a
lower voice.

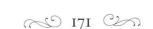

Duchess looked very much alarmed, and continued to scoop the inside of the pie-dish.

"My Great-aunt Squintina (grand-mother of Cousin Tabitha Twitchit) — died of a thimble in a Christmas plum-pudding. *I* never put any article of metal in *my* puddings or pies."

Duchess looked aghast, and tilted up the pie-dish.

"I have only four patty-pans, and they are all in the cupboard."

Duchess set up a howl. "I shall die! I shall die! I have swallowed a patty-pan! Oh, my dear Ribby, I do feel so ill!"

"It is impossible, my dear Duchess; there was not a patty-pan."

Duchess moaned and whined and rocked herself about.

"Oh I feel so dreadful, I have swallowed a patty-pan!"

"There was *nothing* in the pie," said Ribby severely.

"Yes there *was*, my dear Ribby, I am sure I have swallowed it!"

"Let me prop you up with a pillow, my dear Duchess; where do you think you feel it?"

"Oh I do feel so ill *all over* me, my dear Ribby; I have swallowed a large tin patty-pan with a sharp scalloped edge!"

"Shall I run for the doctor? I will just lock up the spoons!"

"Oh yes, yes! fetch Dr. Maggotty, my dear Ribby; he is a Pie himself, he will certainly understand.

Ribby settled Duchess in an armchair before the fire, and went out and hurried to the village to look for the doctor.

She found him at the smithy.

He was occupied in putting rusty nails into a bottle of ink, which he had obtained at the post office.

"Gammon? ha! HA!" said he, with his head on one side.

Ribby explained that her guest had swallowed a patty-pan.

"Spinach? ha! HA!" said he, and accompanied her with alacrity.

He hopped so fast that Ribby had to run. It was most conspicuous. All the village could see that Ribby was fetching the doctor.

"I *knew* they would over-eat themselves!" said Cousin Tabitha Twitchit.

But while Ribby had been hunting for the doctor — a curious thing had happened to Duchess, who had been left by herself, sitting before the fire, sighing and groaning and feeling very unhappy.

"How *could* I have swallowed it! such a large thing as a patty-pan!"

She got up and went to the table, and felt inside the pie-dish again with a spoon.

"No; there is no patty-pan, and I put one in; and nobody has eaten pie except me, so I must have swallowed it!"

She sat down again, and stared mournfully at the grate. The fire crackled and danced, and something sizz-z-zled!

Duchess started! She opened the door of the *top* oven; out came a rich steamy flavour of veal and ham, and there stood a fine brown pie — and through a hole in the top of the pie-crust there was a glimpse of a little tin patty-pan!

Duchess drew a long breath —

"Then I must have been eating Mouse!...No wonder I feel ill...But perhaps I should feel worse if I had really swallowed a patty-pan!" Duchess reflected — "What a very awkward thing to have to explain to Ribby! I think I will put *my* pie in the back-yard and say nothing about it. When I go home, I will run round and take it away." She put it outside the back door, and sat down again by the fire, and shut her eyes; when Ribby arrived with the doctor, she seemed fast asleep.

"Gammon, ha, Ha?" said the doctor.

"I am feeling very much better," said Duchess, waking up with a jump.

"I am truly glad to hear it! He has brought you a pill, my dear Duchess!"

"I think I should feel *quite* well if he only felt my pulse," said Duchess, backing away from the magpie, who sidled up with something in his beak.

"It is only a bread-pill, you had much better take it; drink a little milk, my dear Duchess!"

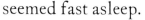

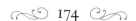

174

"Gammon? Gammon?" said the doctor,
while Duchess coughed and choked.

"Don't say that again!" said Ribby, losing her
temper—"Here, take this bread and jam, and get
out into the yard!"

"Gammon and Spinach! ha ha HA!" shouted
Dr. Maggotty triumphantly outside the back door . . .

"I am feeling very much better, my dear Ribby," said Duchess.
"Do you not think that I had better go home before it gets dark?"

"Perhaps it might be wise, my dear Duchess. I will lend you a nice
warm shawl, and you shall take my arm."

"I would not trouble you for worlds; I feel wonderfully better.
One pill of Dr. Maggotty —"

"Indeed it is most admirable, if it has cured you of a patty-pan!
I will call directly after breakfast to ask how you have slept."

Ribby and Duchess said goodbye affectionately, and Duchess
started home. Half-way up the lane she stopped and looked back;
Ribby had gone in and shut her door. Duchess slipped through
the fence, and ran round to the back of Ribby's house and peeped
into the yard.

Upon the roof of the pig-stye sat Dr. Maggotty and three
jackdaws. The jackdaws were eating pie-crust, and the magpie was
drinking gravy out of a patty-pan.

"Gammon, ha, HA!" he shouted when he saw Duchess's little
black nose peeping round the corner.

Duchess ran home feeling uncommonly silly!

When Ribby came out for a pailful of water to wash up the
tea-things, she found a pink and white pie-dish lying smashed
in the middle of the yard. The patty-pan was under the pump,
where Dr. Maggotty had considerately left it.

Ribby stared with amazement — "Did you ever see the like!

so there really *was* a patty-pan? ... But *my* patty-pans are all in the kitchen cupboard. Well I never did! ... Next time I want to give a party — I will invite Cousin Tabitha Twitchit!"

THE END

THE TALE OF
GINGER AND
PICKLES

™

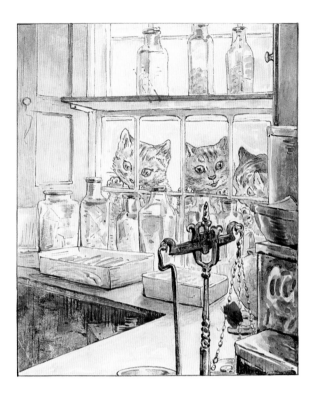

ABOUT THIS BOOK

The Tale of Ginger and Pickles caused much amusement among the villagers of Sawrey when it was published. "It has got a good many views which can be recognized in the village which is what they like," Beatrix wrote to Millie Warne, Harold and Norman's sister. The story also features some familiar friends from previous books, going about their everyday business. Even the policeman from *The Tale of Two Bad Mice* makes an appearance, as do the dolls, Lucinda and Jane.

The book is dedicated to John Taylor, whose wife kept the village shop in Sawrey on which the story-book shop is based. Beatrix had said she couldn't put him in a story as he was always in bed, which explains her dedication, "With very kind regards to old Mr. John Taylor, who 'thinks he might pass as a dormouse!' (Three years in bed and never a grumble!)"

ONCE UPON A TIME there was a village shop. The name over the window was "Ginger and Pickles".

It was a little small shop just the right size for Dolls — Lucinda and Jane Doll-cook always bought their groceries at Ginger and Pickles.

The counter inside was a convenient height for rabbits.

Ginger and Pickles sold red spotty pocket-handkerchiefs at a penny three farthings.

They also sold sugar, and snuff and goloshes.

In fact, although it was such a small shop it sold nearly everything — except a few things that you want in a hurry— like bootlaces, hair-pins and mutton chops.

Ginger and Pickles were the people who kept the shop. Ginger was a yellow tom-cat, and Pickles was a terrier.

The rabbits were always a little bit afraid of Pickles.

The shop was also

patronized by mice —
only the mice were
rather afraid of Ginger.

Ginger usually requested
Pickles to serve them,
because he said it made
his mouth water.

"I cannot bear," said he,
"to see them going out at the
door carrying their little parcels."

"I have the same feeling about
rats," replied Pickles, "but it would never do to eat our
customers; they would leave us and go to Tabitha Twitchit's."

"On the contrary, they would go nowhere," replied Ginger gloomily.

(Tabitha Twitchit kept
the only other shop in
the village. She did
not give credit.)

Ginger and Pickles
gave unlimited credit.

Now the meaning of
"credit" is this — when
a customer buys a bar
of soap, instead of the
customer pulling out a
purse and paying for it —
she says she will pay another time.

And Pickles makes a low bow and says, "With pleasure, madam,"
and it is written down in a book.

The customers come again and again, and buy quantities, in spite
of being afraid of Ginger and Pickles.

But there is no money in what is called the "till".

The customers came in crowds every day and bought quantities, especially the toffee customers. But there was always no money; they never paid for as much as a pennyworth of peppermints.

But the sales were enormous, ten times as large as Tabitha Twitchit's.

As there was always no money, Ginger and Pickles were obliged to eat their own goods.

Pickles ate biscuits and Ginger ate a dried haddock.

They ate them by candle-light after the shop was closed.

When it came to Jan. 1st there was still no money, and Pickles was unable to buy a dog licence.

"It is very unpleasant, I am afraid of the police," said Pickles.

"It is your own fault for being a terrier; *I* do not require a licence, and neither does Kep, the collie dog."

"It is very uncomfortable, I am afraid I shall be summoned. I have tried in vain to get a licence upon credit at the Post Office," said Pickles. "The place is full of policemen. I met one as I was coming home.

"Let us send in the bill again to Samuel Whiskers, Ginger, he owes 22/9 for bacon." "I do not believe that he intends to pay at all," replied Ginger.

"And I feel sure that Anna Maria pockets things — Where are all the cream crackers?"

"You have eaten them yourself," replied Ginger.

Ginger and Pickles retired into the back parlour.

They did accounts. They added up sums and sums, and sums.

"Samuel Whiskers has run up a bill as long as his tail; he has had an ounce and three-quarters of snuff since October.

"What is seven pounds of butter at 1/3, and a stick of sealing wax and four matches?"

"Send in all the bills again to everybody 'with comp^{ts}'," replied Ginger.

After a time they heard a noise in the shop, as if something had been pushed in at the door. They came out of the back parlour. There was an envelope lying on the counter, and a policeman writing in a notebook!

Pickles nearly had a fit, he barked and he barked and made little rushes.

"Bite him, Pickles! bite him!" spluttered Ginger behind a sugar-barrel, "he's only a German doll!"

The policeman went on writing in his notebook; twice he put his pencil in his mouth, and once he dipped it in the treacle.

Pickles barked till he was hoarse. But still the policeman took no notice. He had bead eyes, and his helmet was sewed on with stitches.

At length on his last little rush — Pickles found that the shop was empty. The policeman had disappeared.

But the envelope remained. "Do you think that he has gone to fetch a real live policeman? I am afraid it is a summons," said Pickles.

"No," replied Ginger, who had opened the envelope, "it is the rates and taxes, £3 19 11$^3/_4$."

"This is the last straw," said Pickles, "let us close the shop."

They put up the shutters, and left. But they have not removed from the neighbourhood. In fact some people wish they had gone further.

Ginger is living in the warren. I do not know what occupation he pursues; he looks stout and comfortable.

Pickles is at present a gamekeeper.

The closing of the shop caused great inconvenience. Tabitha Twitchit immediately raised the price of everything a half-penny; and she continued to refuse to give credit.

Of course there are the tradesmen's carts — the butcher, the fishman and Timothy Baker.

But a person cannot live on "seed wigs" and sponge-cake and butter-buns — not even when the sponge-cake is as good as Timothy's!

After a time Mr. John Dormouse and his daughter began to sell peppermints and candles.

But they did not keep "self-fitting sixes"; and it takes five mice to carry one seven-inch candle.

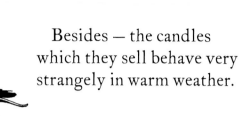

Besides — the candles which they sell behave very strangely in warm weather.

And Miss Dormouse refused to take back the ends when they were brought back to her with complaints.

And when Mr. John Dormouse was complained to, he stayed in bed, and would say nothing but "very snug"; which is not the way to carry on a retail business.

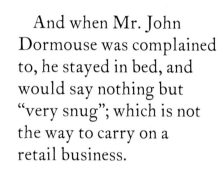

So everybody was pleased when Sally Henny-penny sent out a printed poster to say that she was going to re-open the shop — "Henny's Opening Sale! Grand co-operative Jumble! Penny's penny prices! Come buy, come try, come buy!"

The poster really was most 'ticing.

There was a rush upon the opening day. The shop was crammed with customers, and there were crowds of mice upon the biscuit canisters.

Sally Henny-penny gets rather flustered when she tries to count out change, and she insists on being paid cash; but she is quite harmless.

And she has laid in a remarkable assortment of bargains.

There is something to please everybody.

THE END